Owen w...

By the light [...] Myrddin's R[...] lights were showing, nor could he see Gwen's car, and he wondered where she was.

He was supposed to be home, asleep. But he had awoken with a distinct sense of unease and reached for the gun beside the bed. He had searched the dark until he was convinced that whatever had awakened him wasn't close at hand. Still, he had known that any further attempts at sleep would be futile.

Without pausing to wonder why, he'd come here—only to find Gwen out. Was she with Daniel? The mere thought brought a dangerous light to his eyes. True, she was an independent woman; she had the right to do whatever she pleased. But if she *was* with the lawyer...

His mouth set in a grim line, he settled down to wait until she came home.

Dear Reader,

When two people fall in love, the world is suddenly new and exciting, and it's that same excitement we bring to you in Silhouette Intimate Moments. These are stories with scope, with grandeur. These characters lead the lives we all dream of, and everything they do reflects the wonder of being in love.

Longer and more sensuous than most romances, Silhouette Intimate Moments novels take you away from everyday life and let you share the magic of love. Adventure, glamour, drama, even suspense— these are the passwords that let you into a world where love has a power beyond the ordinary, where the best authors in the field today create stories of love and commitment that will stay with you always.

In coming months look for novels by your favorite authors: Maura Seger, Parris Afton Bonds, Elizabeth Lowell and Erin St. Claire, to name just a few. And whenever you buy books, look for all the Silhouette Intimate Moments, love stories *for* today's women *by* today's women.

Leslie J. Wainger
Senior Editor
Silhouette Books

IMRL-7/85

Maura Seger
Legacy

Silhouette Intimate Moments

Published by Silhouette Books New York

America's Publisher of Contemporary Romance

SILHOUETTE BOOKS
300 East 42nd St., New York, N.Y. 10017

ISBN: 0-373-07194-9

First Silhouette Books printing June 1987

America's Publisher of Contemporary Romance

Printed in the U.S.A.

Books by Maura Seger

Silhouette Special Edition

A Gift Beyond Price #135

Silhouette Intimate Moments

Silver Zephyr #61
Golden Chimera #96
Comes a Stranger #108
Shadows of the Heart #137
Quest of the Eagle #149
Dark of the Moon #162
Happily Ever After #176
Legacy #194

Silhouette Desire

Cajun Summer #282
Treasure Hunt #295

MAURA SEGER

was prompted by a love of books and a vivid imagination to decide, at age twelve, to be a writer. Twenty years later her first book was published. So much, she says, for overnight success! Now each book is an adventure filled with fascinating people who always surprise her.

Chapter 1

It was a country brooded over by mist, half concealing, half revealing a changeable landscape of hills and ravines, fields and lakes. Rock-studded softness of an impossible green. Flashes of slate-gray water lapping at shingle shores.

Here and there the mark of "progress" cut through the bosom of the land, only to give way again as though in shame. Secrets, mysteries, ancient sorrows. A very old place.

Leaning close to the airplane window, Gwen Llywelyn stared out at the land of her forebears, the mystic, mysterious place she had heard of all her life but had never before seen.

Wales. To try not to be affected by its beauty was to attempt the impossible. She could not stand apart from her own sentimentality, so unexpectedly come upon her. Home. It called to something ancient and enduring in her spirit, something that rose up in recognition and rejoiced.

She was not, she was glad to see, alone in her feelings. As the plane touched down at Cardiff and she began gathering up her belongings, she noted in the eyes of several of her fellow passengers the same surprised, grateful, but slightly wary expression she was certain was in her own.

They were all vacationers—as, technically, was she—and they had come expecting no more than a pleasant holiday, only to discover that to retrace the steps of their ancestors demanded more than complacent enjoyment.

It was a subdued group that lined up in front of the Customs desk and offered their passports to be stamped. Never a good traveler, Gwen was tired, grimy and looking forward only to a nice warm bath and a snooze. But her journey was not yet over, and she was beginning to regret the impulse that had made her decide to do it all in a single day.

"Anglesey," she said in response to the Customs officer's question. "I'll be staying on Anglesey."

"A beautiful place," the young man said. "Mam Cymru."

"I beg your pardon?"

He smiled and handed her back her passport. "Mam Cymru. The Mother of Wales. That's what the

island is called. Have a pleasant stay, Miss Llywelyn.''

She nodded, slipped the green booklet back into her
shoulder bag and went to claim her luggage. At the car
rental stand she identified herself, signed the necessary papers and acquired the keys to a compact in the
parking lot. The helpful girl behind the counter
marked the route for her on a map.

''I don't think you'll get lost, Miss. You'll be following the coast heading west, then north. You should
reach Anglesey by late afternoon.''

Gwen thanked her and headed outside. The mid-
morning air was cool and damp, for all that it was
summer. Beneath the smell of diesel fumes that hung
around every airport she caught the faint but stubborn whiff of new-mown grass and flowers, the tang
of salt air.

Clouds skittered across an azure sky. She heard the
laughter of children in short pants running ahead of
patient parents, the eager chatter of reunited families,
the excited conversation of passengers setting out for
parts unknown. Contentment eased her weariness.

She pushed the trolley with her luggage into the
parking lot, found her car and quickly loaded the
trunk. In her purse was the letter from her great-aunt's
solicitor. She mentally reviewed it as she turned the key
in the ignition and started on her way.

She had never met Daniel Pierce, but through their
correspondence she felt that she had come to know
him. He had the dry, precise manner of lawyers

everywhere, but with a touch of lyricism that was purely Welsh. He had written in his first letter:

I regret to inform you of the death of your great-aunt, Miss Winifred Llywelyn, who passed away on this Friday last. Please be assured that her going was peaceful. As she was an elderly lady, some ninety-three years of age, and of a practical turn of mind, she left careful instructions for her burial, which took place Monday last. In her village of Castell Myrddin she was held in universal respect and affection. There was a good turnout.

As Miss Llywelyn's sole living relative, you are heir to the house and surrounding lands, known as Myrddin's Rock. Please advise this office as to what disposition you would like made. A letter from Miss Llywelyn to you, which we were instructed to deliver at this time, is enclosed.

In the letter the far-off voice of a woman Gwen would now never meet had spoken with quiet matter-of-factness. Winifred wrote:

I know that this must all come as a great surprise to you, since the two branches of our family have had little contact over the years. But it is my hope that before deciding what to do with Myrddin's Rock you will come and see it for yourself. I have spent all my life here with great joy, and regret only the leaving of it. It is not impossible that you might find the same happiness.

Gwen doubted it. She was happy enough in her life, having worked hard to earn her position as assistant curator of medieval art at Harvard's Busch-Reisinger Museum. Her apartment in Cambridge was small but homey; she had enough good friends never to feel alone in the world; and she was one of those rare women who was satisfied with her appearance, finding herself neither too fat nor too thin.

Men had a tendency to tell her that she was beautiful, which she discounted with the healthy skepticism that served her well in all parts of life. She saw nothing particularly outstanding about golden red hair, large gray eyes and delicate features. After all, she had been looking at them all her life.

But that didn't mean that at twenty-nine she was immune to the lure of an adventure. With more than a month's vacation time accumulated, she intended to enjoy herself. She would get to know Wales, dispose of her inheritance and perhaps even give some thought as to what to do about Jeffrey.

She smiled wryly to herself. The year before there had been a well-publicized survey released by Yale University, showing that a woman who hadn't married by the time she was thirty had a steadily decreasing chance of ever doing so.

The survey had caused considerable comment among Gwen's friends; a few revealed something close to panic as they thought of time running out, but most stalwartly defended their ability to get along fine without a man.

Gwen didn't fall into either category. She wanted to marry—someday—and to have children, but she felt no sense of desperation because she hadn't done so already. Which perhaps explained why she continued to hold Jeffrey at arm's length.

Traffic beyond the airport grew heavier as she slipped into what passed for the morning rush hour in Cardiff, and she was distracted from her thoughts by the need to concentrate on her driving. Staying to the left side of the road was more difficult than she had expected, and she was relieved to leave the city behind.

The countryside unfolded majestically, haunting in its beauty and in the unexpected thoughts it provoked. She was glad of the all but empty road as she found herself wondering about the people of her own blood who had once lived on the land she now sped through. She knew little about them except what a few family names, a handful of precious sepia photographs and a confused smattering of stories that seemed more like legends, could reveal.

All she really knew was that her grandfather had left Wales some seventy-five years before, apparently convinced that there was no future for him as a younger son who would not inherit. He had been a gentle, scholarly man who worked a variety of odd jobs to put himself through school, eventually becoming a professor of history. His only son, Gwen's father, had become a doctor, and Gwen herself had never doubted that education was the route to both success and happiness.

That much at least she had in common with the grandfather who had died before her birth. But whether she would also find any bond with the home that had once been his and that, due to a strange twist of fate, had become hers, she could not say.

Anglesey, the island for which she was bound, lay off the northwest coast of Wales. By the time she reached the bridge connecting it to the mainland, she was feeling the full effects of her long trip. Not even the fresh breeze off the Irish Sea managed to revive her more than marginally.

In the fading light of afternoon, the island appeared bathed in gold. From a distant glen a shimmering rainbow arched. Gwen traced its path across the sky and knew an odd rush of pleasure. Surely it was only her fatigue that made her feel even more strongly than before that she was no stranger here, but rather a journeyer coming at last, gratefully, home.

The feeling persisted as she left the bridge and drove north toward the small village of Castell Myrddin. The lawyer's instructions were precise; she had no difficulty finding the house, although at first glance she thought she must surely have made a mistake.

Whatever she had expected to find at the end of the long dirt path that turned off the main road, it wasn't this. A farmhouse, perhaps, or maybe even a glorified manor. Not a rough-hewn round tower attached to a low stone building, both lacking in even the rudiments of architectural attractiveness, having been built for the sole purpose of defense.

Technically, she was looking at a castle, though it bore no resemblance whatsoever to the fanciful crenellated creations of the late Middle Ages, complete with banners flying and fair maidens sighing. This was a harsh structure for a harsh land, a place where it was possible to believe that generations of Llywelyns had fought a stark battle for survival against often immense odds.

Yet Great-Aunt Winifred had been happy here. Clearly there was no accounting for taste. Gingerly Gwen eased open the heavy wooden door with the key Mr. Pierce had thoughtfully left under the milk can. Beyond were shadows and the smell of damp stone.

That was hardly surprising, since directly below the house she could hear the clash of waves against the shore. Myrddin's Rock was perched on a cliff overlooking a cove. A narrow beach formed a tightly arched crescent directly beneath the leaded windows that grudgingly admitted light. Gwen peered through them with equal reluctance. She didn't even want to imagine what the place was like during a storm.

Suppressing a sigh, she made a quick survey of the rooms in the lower part of the building. The walls were very thick and the ceilings low, the stone floors sloped in places where generations of feet had trod trenches. If the Llywelyns had ever felt an impulse to soften their surroundings and make them more comfortable, they had stalwartly resisted it.

The downstairs consisted only of a primitive kitchen, a small sitting room and a darkly paneled space that might once have been a dining hall. The furniture, what there was of it, was worn, but more comfortable than appearances indicated. The rooms themselves were meticulously clean, but had an air of recent disuse that made her think again of Winifred.

She returned to the car and removed her luggage. With a suitcase in each hand she began to climb the steep stone steps of the tower. There was no railing, but even if there had been, she wouldn't have been able to hold on. Normally there was nothing wrong with her balance, but now an unpleasant sense of dizziness swept over her, until it seemed as though the sea were growing ever louder, pounding against the thick, salt-pitted walls.

Not until she reached the first landing and paused to look back down did she realize that the tightly curling staircase held between smooth stone walls resembled the inner passages of a shell in which sound became trapped. The sea was a living presence in the house, and had been for centuries. It was a far more permanent resident than she could ever expect to be.

"Your imagination's running away with you," she grumbled to herself. Her voice bounced off the walls, echoing faintly all the way down, discouraging her from speaking again.

Off the first landing was an iron-studded door that led to a surprisingly pleasant bedroom. Gwen took one look at it and decided it would suit her fine, and that the rest of the tower could wait to be explored. Particularly since she glimpsed a small bathroom off to the side, complete with a claw-footed tub and a hot water tank suspended from the ceiling.

Half an hour later, floating in the tub, she leaned back and smiled blissfully. So the house wasn't what she had expected. So what? She was hardly too set in her ways to appreciate a surprise—at least as long as she could soak away the stiffness of her trip and look forward to a good night's sleep.

It was barely early evening, the start of the long Celtic twilight, when she emerged from the tub and toweled herself dry. The free-standing mirror in a carved oak frame showed a young woman with smooth, pale skin, full breasts, a slender waist and rounded hips. Her legs were long and firm, her carriage erect, her posture instinctively proud.

Wrapped in a blue silk robe, she brushed her hair until it lay in shining disarray around her shoulders. Accepting that it wasn't going to behave, she left it and padded barefoot down the stairs, finding them less intimidating this time.

The kitchen was stocked, not with an overabundance of food, but with everything she needed for the next few days. Once again Mr. Pierce had come through. She made a mental note to thank him as she fixed herself a sandwich of thickly sliced chicken on fresh brown bread.

She was perched on a stool by the window, overlooking a carefully tended herb garden, when she stopped in midbite and stared. Not twenty feet away a man stood silhouetted against the setting sun. She could make out little about him except that he was tall and broad shouldered, and held one arm outstretched, crooked at the elbow.

There was a sudden flurry of wings, a flash of gleaming talons, and a large bird settled onto his arm. The man inclined his head, and she thought he murmured to the bird, though she couldn't hear him. The bird preened and suffered its breast to be stroked.

Over the feral head set off by a lethal beak, her startled eyes met the man's. He paused, but barely. Before she could think to move, he strode briskly toward the house. Not for nothing had Gwen lived most of her life in and near big cities. She knew perfectly well that a woman alone did not encourage strangers to drop by. Particularly not large, male ones with unusual pets.

But there was nothing to be done for it. The knock on the kitchen door was far too brisk and authoritative to brook refusal. Reluctantly she put her forgotten sandwich down and went to answer it.

"Yes?" she inquired cautiously, having eased the door open a scant few inches.

The man stood with his feet planted firmly apart, his head tilted arrogantly. His hair was so darkly ebony that the fading light cast silver glints through it. His face was square, with a broad forehead, assertive nose and firm chin. Gwen was struck by the clarity and power of his eyes, as blue as the sky had been earlier and deeply set beneath thick black brows. The left brow was broken by a thin white scar that ran upward toward his hairline.

Without preamble he demanded, "Who would you happen to be?"

Gwen had never been easily intimidated. Life as an only child had taught her to look after herself from an early age. Confronted by the stranger, she stiffened her back and answered him in kind. "Why should I tell you?"

He looked startled. Clearly people did not usually have the nerve to respond to him like that. Having little experience with it, he also had little patience. "For the love of—"

"Go away."

She moved to shut the door, only to be stopped when he jammed his foot firmly inside. A moment later he had followed, the bird still perched on his arm. Both were glowering at her.

"Now just a minute," she tried, appalled when her voice squeaked. This was more than she had bargained for.

She was vainly wishing she had taken the self-defense course a friend of hers had tried to get her to sign up for, when he said disdainfully, "I've heard of people doing this, but I never thought that anyone would have the nerve.''

Gwen took a deep breath and cleared her throat. He was a nut, a gorgeous one, but still a nut. Of course, maybe being born with fabulously rugged features, nonstop shoulders, a chest to dream on and all the other accoutrements of a perfectly formed male had that effect on a man. Certainly he gave every evidence of being accustomed to getting his way. But she was just as determined not to give it to him.

''If you are not out of here in ten seconds,'' she said, ''I'm calling my husband. The ex-Green Beret.''

''Fine, then I'll have a word with him about what *he's* doing here, too.''

Perhaps he thought it was his house. People came down with delusions like that all the time. Not anyone she knew, of course, but surely people somewhere did.

''Look,'' she said, trying hard to be reasonable, ''my name is Gwen Llywelyn, and I live here. At least, right now I do. I inherited the house from my Great-Aunt Winifred.''

''Good Lord.'' His eyes bored into hers. Even the bird, which she had calmed down enough to recognize as a falcon, looked interested.

''I'm sorry if that upsets you.''

''Winny said you'd come, but I thought that was wishful thinking.''

''Winny?'' He had known her great-aunt, presumably even been friends with her? Or maybe he was just trying to lull her into a false sense of security before he...

"You're young."

"Not too." She squared her shoulders and straightened to her full five-and-a-half feet in height, which still left her considerably short of his six feet plus. "And I assure you, I'm perfectly capable of looking after myself."

"With the help of the ex-Green Beret husband? Awfully quiet, isn't he? Perhaps he's napping. By the way, mind if I put Alexander down?"

"Alexander...?"

"The falcon. He's used to perching on Winny's kitchen chairs. Don't worry, he won't scratch them." True to the stranger's word, the bird looked utterly guileless when he was lowered to the back of one of the chairs.

"I'm Owen Garrett," the man said, holding out a hand exactly as though they were meeting at some very proper Cambridge cocktail party. "Your neighbor."

"Why do I have the feeling there's more to it than that?" Which begged the larger question of why the mere touch of his fingers against hers turned her heart into a trip-hammer and made her feel absurdly giddy. Almost as she had on the stairs, only worse, because this time there was no excuse.

"Because you're very suspicious?" he ventured amiably. "I've noticed that about Americans. They tend to either overwhelm you with friendliness right off the bat or be so wary that you can't get close to them.''

"That's a generalization. We're individuals, like everyone else."

He smiled, a deep, slow smile that revealed evenly spaced white teeth, which, again absurdly, made her think of the falcon...hunting. "You certainly are, Gwen Llywelyn. Though you look a bit the way Winny did when she was young."

"How would you know that?" Despite herself, her curiosity was caught. It wasn't only that he was so attractive and did such strange things to her equilibrium; she had the sense of keen intelligence lurking behind the sapphire eyes, and of a kind of strength she hadn't encountered very often before, if ever.

"I've seen pictures of her. They're around here somewhere. She was really something, was Winny. By the way, would you have any beer?"

"If you'd like a drink..." She thought she hit just the right note, managing to sound not too encouraging, but not inhospitable, either. The man was probably used to having women jump through hoops for him. Better that he should find out she was different right from the start.

"It's for Alexander. He likes something after a long flight."

"Oh, then by all means." She got a bottle of lager from the refrigerator and, following Owen's instructions, poured a small amount into a bowl, which she placed on the table near Alexander's chair. He bobbed his head to her, hopped over and helped himself.

"What an unusual bird."

"Not really. Falcons have lived around people for so long that they've picked up some of our habits."

"Perhaps you'd like the rest of this," she said, indicating the half-filled bottle.

"I wouldn't mind, if you'll join me."

As she fetched two glasses and another bottle, he settled his long frame into a chair and watched her. His gaze was disconcertingly steady, and he felt no need to cover it with chitchat. She became uncomfortably aware of her rather informal state, but resisted the impulse to pull her robe more tightly together.

"Came over from America, did you?" he inquired pleasantly when she had joined him at the table.

"From Boston."

"With the husband."

"Actually..." Gwen rarely tried to lie; it simply wasn't in her. She'd had no idea what that lack of practice meant until she actually made the attempt.

"There isn't one," he said helpfully.

She flushed and looked away. "Was it that obvious?"

"No ring."

"Some women don't wear them these days."

He shrugged, managing with that simple gesture to communicate his utter disdain for any man who would permit such an aberration. The muscles of his throat worked as he took a long swallow of the lager. His white cotton shirt was open for several buttons, which seemed to be missing, anyway. It went with his faded corduroy slacks, which were tucked into old but cared-for boots.

It occurred to her that in this neck of the woods he was probably a farmer. Which meant, almost inevitably, that he had very little money. Unlike Jeffrey, who was positively rolling in it, and tended to depend on that to too large a degree. Gwen pulled her attention back to the matter at hand.

"Look," she said, "I'm sorry if I seemed standoffish at first. But being here alone and having you turn up all of a sudden..."

"Quite all right. I understand. But now that you know who I am..."

"I don't really."

Dark brows drew together in a frown. "But I told you."

"Your name and that you knew Winny. You could tell me anything, though, and I wouldn't know if it was true or not. I never met my great-aunt, and I had no idea this place was going to be left to me. I only arrived a few hours ago, and I haven't even seen the lawyer yet, so..."

"Pierce." He was scowling.

"Yes, he's been very helpful."

"He would be."

"What's that supposed to mean?"

"Forget it." He stood abruptly and held out his arm. Alexander left his perch and, without moving his wings that Gwen could see, crossed the distance between them as though gravity no longer existed. "You're thinking of selling."

Taken aback by his abrupt change in manner, she didn't known how to respond, except to tell the truth. "I don't see what it has to do with you, but yes, I am."

"You won't."

"I beg your pardon?"

Owen turned to go. "Just as I said. You won't sell."

"I hardly think you have any reason to believe that."

He looked back at her over his broad shoulder, and his expression was suddenly less accusing, gentler. "Get some sleep, Gwen Llywelyn. You look done in."

"Thanks very much."

The tart edge of her tongue didn't faze him. He merely smiled. "And very lovely. I'm glad the husband isn't real."

She opened her mouth to make some appropriate retort, only to close it when she realized he was already gone.

Chapter 2

The village of Castell Myrddin was nestled between two squat granite peaks that loomed over it protectively. It was within sight of the all-pervasive sea, but, unlike the tower, sheltered enough to seem a solid part of the land. The main street ran the length of two Boston city blocks and was dotted with shops that looked not so much quaint as merely suitable to where and what they happened to be.

A handful of cars, mostly older models, were parked along the street, and perhaps a dozen people were out and about. They eyed Gwen cautiously and, in response to her direct, friendly gaze, inclined their heads. A few even smiled back.

She was satisfied with that, having taken it for granted that country people weren't really likely to be all that different from city folks, even in another country. Everyone was cautious these days, and strangers were always suspect until proven otherwise.

She supposed it wouldn't be long before word of why she was there got around, and she wondered what the reaction would be. Old friends of Winny's might seek her out, and she hoped that not too many would react as Owen Garrett had.

Throughout the previous night, when she should have been sleeping off her trip, he had occupied far too much of her thoughts. The man had a nerve storming into her house, frightening her, then daring to suggest that she didn't know her own mind. Of course she was going to sell, the sooner the better.

Daniel Pierce was glad to hear that. When she had climbed the stairs to his second-floor office above the dry goods store, he greeted her with an eager hand-shake, a broad smile and a cup of strong tea.

"I've coffee if you prefer," he offered, "but to be honest, it probably wouldn't be what you're used to."

"Tea is fine," she assured him, having been seated in a wide leather armchair across from his paper-strewn desk. His office reminded her of the inner sanctums of certain absentminded professors she knew in Cambridge. But there was nothing vague about the man himself.

He was younger than she had expected, not more than forty, and well-built in a slender, wiry way. His hair was blond, combed straight back from a high forehead and a shade longer than might be thought strictly proper by people who worried about such things. He wore a gray three-piece suit with a blue shirt, but had taken the jacket off and rolled up his sleeves. Carbon paper had smudged his right arm.

"There you are," he said as he handed her the cup. "Now tell me, did you have a good journey?"

"Good enough," she said with a smile. "I don't really like flying."

He nodded. "I'm a train man myself, or, failing that, give me a boat. Never saw the sense of being cooped up in a tin can that really has no business being where it is."

Gwen agreed and felt an instant rapport with him. "At any rate, I got here, and now I'd like to talk with you about Myrddin's Rock."

"Ah, yes. What do you think of it?"

She smiled faintly. "It's not what I . . . expected."

Daniel nodded. "I thought of writing to you, explaining what it looked like, but then I decided it would be best for you to form your own opinion."

"Don't misunderstand me, in some ways it's lovely."

"Oh, yes, beautiful location, for one thing. And then there's a certain historical significance. Some people like that sort of thing."

"Then you don't think there will be any trouble selling?"

"Well . . ." He leaned back in his chair and pressed his fingers together, looking at her over them. "I wouldn't say the market for such a house is huge, but with persistence it should be possible to get a fairly decent price. If you like, I could look into it for you.''

"I'd appreciate that.'' She felt compelled to add, "It's not that I wouldn't like to keep it. It's just that with my life in the States..."

"Of course. I quite understand. And I'm sure Winny would have, too.''

"Actually,'' Gwen said, "I feel a little uncomfortable about that. The letter you forwarded made it clear that she hoped I would keep the house.''

He took a sip of his tea and bobbed his head. "Winny would have liked that, no doubt. But she was a very sensible woman, and I'm sure she understood that you have a life of your own.''

Soothed by his reassurance, Gwen allowed herself to be persuaded. "Well,'' she said as she set her cup down, "if you'll draw up the necessary papers for me, I'll be around for the next few weeks to sign them. I don't expect this to be wrapped up by then, so I thought I'd give you my power of attorney, or whatever you call it over here, and you can handle everything for me.''

"I appreciate your confidence,'' he said, rising as she did. "And, I assure you, you won't be disappointed. It may take a while to effect a sale, but in the meantime there are sufficient funds to pay for the upkeep of the house. You won't be out-of-pocket.''

Gwen hadn't thought of that and was glad of his practicality. She also felt good about Daniel Pierce himself, despite Owen's slighting reference. He struck her as a sensible, dependable man.

"By the way," he said as he was showing her out, "seeing as how you are a stranger to these parts, perhaps you'd like to see something of them. I'd be pleased to show you around."

"That's very kind of you," Gwen said, "but I wouldn't want to take you away from your family."

Apparently the code phrases that were understood in Cambridge were just as current on Anglesey. For family, read wife.

He smiled, appreciating her tact. "I don't have one, so perhaps you'd consider letting me by your guide."

Relieved, she nodded. "I'd be delighted." Actually, she had been wondering how she was going to occupy her time, and his offer solved that problem. Moreover, she genuinely thought she would enjoy his company. He was certainly much more what she was used to then Owen Garrett.

That thought prompted her to say, "By the way, I had a visitor yesterday. A man named Owen Garrett showed up at my kitchen door. I take it he lives nearby." Her choice of words was deliberate, downplaying the event and suggesting that she had been no more than mildly put out by it.

Daniel reacted more strongly. He frowned and looked concerned. "Unfortunately he does. He didn't make a pest of himself, did he?"

"No, though he did seem to have some firm ideas about Myrddin's Rock."

"Unfortunate. Winny encouraged him, you see. She felt sorry for him, I suppose, or was simply too tenderhearted to turn him away."

That was so far at odds with Gwen's impression of her visitor that she was prompted to ask, "What on earth for?"

Daniel sighed, his gray eyes shadowed. "I'm afraid Owen fancies himself a throwback of sorts. He's one of those romantics who despises the modern Wales and believes that the distant past was vastly better than the present. A proponent of the Camelot myth would probably be the best way to put it."

"You mean King Arthur, the round table, all that stuff?"

He nodded. "Very picturesque, of course, but it has nothing to do with the real world. Not that people like Owen will ever admit it. He dabbles in legend and myth, keeps falcons, collects old weapons, that sort of thing."

It sounded rather interesting to Gwen, particularly given her own background in medieval art. But she had to admit that, the way Daniel put it, Owen didn't seem to be too tightly wrapped.

"How does he support himself?" she asked. "Does he farm?"

"Not really. I'm not sure what he does for money. Of course, he was great friends with Winny, and she had a bit squirreled away."

Implicit in that was a suggestion Gwen didn't care for. Surely Owen hadn't been taking advantage of her great-aunt's kindness and perhaps thinking that he could do the same with her? If so, he was in for a rude awakening.

Gwen's family prided itself on hard work and self-discipline, and gave generously to charity. But she was not about to let anyone stand by and make a patsy of her. A healthy, strong man like Owen was more than capable of supporting himself, if he only put his mind to it.

"If he keeps pestering you," Daniel said as he held the door for her, "tell me, and I'll take care of it."

She resisted the impulse to look skeptical, well aware that in sheer physical size the two men were hardly evenly matched. More than that, there was a sense of barely restrained power about Owen that Daniel couldn't hope to equal. It was the difference, she told herself, between a truly civilized man and one who preferred to live in a far more violent past.

"Thanks," she said, "but I'd just as soon forget about him."

Daniel looked undeniably pleased. He pressed her hand for a moment longer than he absolutely had to and said, "I'll call you tomorrow."

Fine with her, except that when she got home—there she was, thinking of it that way again—she discovered that the phone wasn't working and the kitchen sink had sprung a leak. A quick look underneath the latter strongly suggested that Great-Aunt Winny had been no stranger to plumbing problems.

Living as she did in a converted town house, Gwen had done her share of repairs. She quickly located a wrench and set to with a will, soon satisfying herself that at least she wasn't going to be flooded out.

The phone was a bigger problem. Even if she had known whom to call to report it, she couldn't have. She could drive back into the village, except that a glance at her watch told her that the shops would be closing. She hadn't noticed any pay phones, and had no reason to think Daniel would still be in his office. Which left her with only one alternative.

"I don't even know where he lives," she muttered to herself even as she remembered seeing Owen cut toward the west when he had left the house the previous evening. From the way Daniel had talked, he couldn't live too far away.

If nothing else, a little walk would do her good. She added a light jacket to her linen slacks and silk shirt, checked to make sure she had her key and left the house.

A gravel path ran nearby, disappearing over a hillock. Following it, she paused to look at the sea, azure in the late afternoon sunlight that lit a sky that seemed to go on forever. Far off in the distance was Ireland, but she could see only the misty haze of a horizon that lent itself to imagined wonders.

With very little effort she cast her mind back to the days when Viking longships had plowed these waters, bringing terror to those who saw them, and a barbaric vitality to the history they helped to shape. This land had been fought over since ancient times, stained with blood, hallowed with cries, yet always retaining a majestic strength that hinted at forces far beyond the power of man.

When she reached the coolness of a hidden glen she could understand how the legends of fairy folk had come to be. They were a reasonable explanation for powers people sensed but could not grasp, as was the tale of Arthur, a mixture of the true and the fantastic, reality and dreams.

Did Owen understand the difference? Daniel had suggested strongly that he didn't. There was a rivalry between the two men that puzzled her. They were so different, and seemingly part of such different spheres of existence, that she couldn't imagine how or why they should clash.

Unless Owen was simply one of those people who needed no excuse to pick a quarrel. He had seemed rather volatile the evening before. She paused, wondering just how important it was to get the phone fixed. Perhaps she could wait a while, except that she really didn't like the idea of being so cut off.

She kept going and, over the rise of the next hill, spotted a long, low stone building built around a center courtyard and topped on one side by a graceful bell tower. Next to it were a well-kept garden and orchards; nearby were pens that held several contented-looking sheep and goats. Behind the building a fenced pasture ran down toward the sea. Gwen's breath caught as she saw the magnificent stallion grazing there.

The sharp thud of metal on metal brought her attention to a small wooden building a short distance from the main house. An overhang obscured the entrance, but within the shadows she could see the red-orange glow of fire.

Cautiously she made her way down the hill and across a neatly swept open space until she was close enough to see inside. The fire leaped in a stone pit raised above the hard packed earth floor. It glowed like the eye of an irate dragon and sent wisps of smoke through an opening in the ceiling.

Resting on the edge of the pit and hanging from hooks all through the shed were metal implements that looked as though they belonged in the tool bag of a medieval torturer. There were long-handled prongs and pliers, mallets and wrenches, and ominous-appearing gadgets whose purpose she could not guess.

Then she reined in her imagination and realized that she was looking at nothing more esoteric than a smithy's shed. A stack of carefully curved horseshoes lay off to one side near what appeared to be a half-completed chandelier of wrought iron.

She stepped forward to admire the delicately crafted object, when a sudden sound drew her back. Owen came around the corner, carrying a bucket of water, and paused when he saw her.

"I should have knocked," she murmured, staring at him.

His gaze was equally intent. "That's all right. I just wasn't expecting company."

Obviously, since he was stripped to the waist, his bronzed skin streaked with sweat and his hair falling in damp ebony curls over his forehead. Bared, his shoulders appeared even broader than they had the day before, and were suited to the wide but graceful breadth of his chest, which carried not an ounce of flab. A dark line of hair spanned the distance between his flat nipples and arched downward over the hard ridge of his abdomen.

The pair of worn jeans slung low on his narrow hips did little to hide the sinewy strength of his lower body. His thighs looked rock hard, and she was left in no doubt as to his virility. He was all supple muscle, sun-honed skin and masculine strength, stripped of any pretense of civilization.

Gwen's tongue darted out to moisten lips that had gone suddenly dry. She felt at once schoolgirl-foolish and woman-wise. Having never been prey to more than a mild appreciation of a good male physique, she was stunned by the impact he had on her. Surely she wasn't turning into one of those shallow creatures whose head could be turned by a handsome face or other, more basic, attributes.

"Look," she said nervously, "if it isn't convenient, I'll go. I don't want to disturb you."

Owen frowned. She was doing just that, and the thought of her leaving hardly helped. He had been thinking about her far too much since the previous day, hence his decision to tackle some good, hard physical work in the hope that it would clear his mind.

It hadn't. Upon first entering the blacksmith shed and seeing her standing there, he had seriously thought for a moment that he might be hallucinating. She looked so damn lovely in whatever she was wearing, those soft, clingy things that emphasized the gentle curves of her body.

Her hair was pulled up off her long, graceful neck, but tendrils had come loose and now spilled around the oval purity of her face. Against the red glow of the fire her alabaster skin shone like polished ivory, and the gray depths of her eyes were touched with green that reminded him of a forest glen at dawn.

"It's not important," he said, setting down the bucket. "I was planning to quit soon, anyway, and get something to eat. Would you care to join me?"

"Actually, I only came over to ask if I could use the phone. Mine is out of order." Not that she wasn't tempted to seize any pretext for staying longer. Far too tempted.

"That happens all the time," he said as he reached for a shirt hanging from a nearby hook. He put it on but didn't bother to button it, so it hung open outside his jeans. She tried hard not to stare at the expanse of chest that was still revealed to her.

"What does?" she murmured absently.

"The phone going out. If yours is, chances are mine is, too. But you're welcome to check."

She nodded, and together they walked back toward the larger building, keeping a cautious distance from each other. The closer they got to the low stone structure with the bell tower, the bigger it appeared, until she felt curious enough to ask, "Do you live here by yourself?"

"If you don't count Alexander, three other falcons, Wind Dancer—that's the horse you probably already saw—and a temperamental sheepdog named Lancelot."

"It must be quite a lot for one person to care for."

"It was a wreck when I found it. Restoring it fully will take years yet."

She could appreciate that when they stepped inside through iron-studded double doors. The interior was cool and slightly damp, redolent of the smell she could associate only with great age. It was as though time itself had seeped into the place and become part of its very mortar.

Outside it had been quiet enough, but inside there was a deep hush that made her instinctively hold her breath. "What was this place?" she asked in little more than a whisper.

"Before it was abandoned, it served as a barn and stable. But originally, going back centuries, it was a monastery."

Yes, that fit. There was an air of sanctity that no amount of time could destroy. She had little difficulty imagining orderly rows of brown clad, hooded men going about their chores, offering up the simplest service to the greater glory of their Maker.

What was incongruous was that Owen should choose to live in such a place, and to labor over it so lovingly. For she could think of no other description suited to the restoration he had already done. Beyond the shadowed entry hall she could see the courtyard garden, vibrant with summer flowers and fragrant herbs. A marble fountain filled with splashing water shone in the sun. Gravel paths were weeded and raked.

"How lovely," she said, almost to herself. This was a place for contemplation, serene thought, dreaming. A sanctuary from the rough and tumble of the world. She couldn't help but wonder what had prompted him to create it for himself.

"Let me show you around," he said with boyish enthusiasm. "This wing is almost finished."

It consisted of a long, high-ceilinged room with a massive fireplace at one end, which she guessed must once have been the refectory. Next to it, down a short flight of steps, well worn in the center, was the kitchen. At first glance it looked untouched by modern hands. There was a large wooden worktable in the center. Baskets held dried herbs, onions and other supplies. Open wooden shelves contained brass and tin implements, as well as dry goods. Above a stone basin was what appeared to be the sole source of water, a hand-operated pump.

"How...picturesque," she murmured, wondering how anyone managed to cook in such a place. Her idea of preparing a meal was to pop something into the microwave or, if she was feeling especially creative, whip something up in the food processor.

"It's not as bad as it looks," Owen said with a grin. He opened a door off to the side and gave her a glimpse of a large pantry, complete with refrigerator and freezer. "Most of the house isn't electrified, and I'm probably going to leave it that way, but I did run wiring into here and a couple of other rooms. Call it a compromise, if you will.

"The phone," he added, gesturing back up the stairs, "is through there."

Off the refectory was a small room that might once have served the abbot and that was now Owen's library and den. A heavily carved mahogany table, such as might have belonged to a Renaissance prince, was clear of all but a lamp, a neat stack of papers and a pen. Bookshelves lined the room. There was a comfortable chair with a side table beside it, on which rested the phone.

Owen picked it up, listened for a moment and shrugged. "As I thought, it's out, too. But don't worry. The phone company will probably have the trouble fixed in a few days."

"Days," she repeated. "Can't they do it any sooner?"

He smiled gently. "Things tend to move slower here than I expect you're used to. Besides, what's the urgency? You can get by without a phone."

He was right, of course, except that in her modern world people were always linked, however tenuously. They never had to depend completely on themselves.

Owen saw the look of concern that flashed across her face and guessed at its cause. He thought it rather endearing that a woman of such apparent strength and independence should be prey to such fears, until it occurred to him that he might be the source of her anxiety.

As if to confirm that, she glanced toward the door. "I'd better be going."

"There's no need. As I said, you're welcome to join me for supper."

"I wouldn't want to impose."

She hesitated just enough to convince him that she really did want to stay. He smiled his relief. "Give me a few minutes to get cleaned up." As he strode from the room he added, "Make yourself comfortable."

It didn't seem possible that she could do that, not with such strange feelings flitting through her. She needed a distraction from the emotions he made her feel. She glanced at the bookshelves, only to have her attention instantly caught.

Owen's tastes were extensive and wide-ranging. He apparently enjoyed everything from modern novels and works of history and biography to hand-tooled leather volumes dating from past centuries, written not only in English but also in French, German and what she could only suppose was Welsh.

To her delight she found among his collection the works of her favorite medievalist, James Owens, a renowned Oxford scholar whose analyses of life in preindustrial Britain bristled with wit and insight. He had also authored an immensely popular study of parallels between the pestilence-ridden fourteenth century and the nuclear era, which had sat on all the bestseller lists for more than a year.

She was curled up in the overstuffed chair, enjoying the insights of a brilliant, articulate mind, when Owen returned. It took her a moment to finish the paragraph she'd been immersed in and look up at him.

He had showered, and his thick hair was still damp with diamond-drops of moisture. The worn jeans had been replaced by tailored corduroy trousers, and his chest was discreetly—if no less impressively—covered by a cotton sweater. He glanced at the book she was reading and frowned slightly. "Not really good on an empty stomach, wouldn't you say?"

She put it aside and rose. "Actually, I can read him anytime. He's incredibly exciting."

Owen didn't comment further, but stood aside to let her precede him from the room. She caught a whiff of sun-warmed skin and clean, uncomplicated soap. In the kitchen he gestured her to a chair at the table before matter-of-factly beginning to assemble the ingredients for a meal. He didn't ask for her help, nor did he show any sign of needing it. Clearly he was a man as comfortable looking after himself in the kitchen as he was everywhere else.

"That's an odd way to describe a historian," he said as he got two cold beers from the refrigerator and poured them into frosted tankards. "Sounds more suited to a pop star."

"I suppose it's a matter of what appeals to you," she said after taking a sip. "I've always been more attracted to a man's mind than to, uh, anything else."

His dark eyebrows rose fractionally. "Really? I'll have to remember that."

There was a moment's silence during which she wondered what on earth had prompted her to make such a comment. That it was true didn't explain why she had turned the conversation in such a potentially dangerous direction. The last thing she wanted was to discuss personal matters with Owen.

His lean, browned hands built a fire in the wood stove with practiced ease. When it was going to his satisfaction he used a razor-sharp knife to cut almost impossibly thin potato slices which he then tossed in a skillet of heated oil. They fried in seconds, and he lifted them out, depositing the growing heap on an earthenware platter covered with paper towels. As he worked he asked, seemingly in passing, "How did you and Pierce hit it off?"

"Fine." Only after she had answered did it occur to her that there was anything noteworthy about his question. "But how did you know I'd seen him?"

He shrugged and disappeared into the pantry. When he returned, carrying a folded gunnysack, he said,

"Castell Myrddin is a small town. A village, really. Any visitor is going to be an object of interest."

"In other words, be gossiped about."

Unwrapping the sack to reveal two plump, glistening trout, he said, "It goes with the territory. There's nothing malicious about it."

She could have commented further, but instead chose to see if she couldn't throw him as far off base as he had her. Casually she said, "There's something I've noticed about you. When you speak, you use a fair number of Americanisms, such as what you just said about it going with the territory. You wouldn't be American by any chance, would you?"

He laughed and shook his head. "No, I'm Welsh all the way through, but I did go to school over there. That undoubtedly accounts for my eclectic vocabulary."

She wanted to ask which school, and for what, but before she could do so, he changed the subject again. "You didn't tell me, what do you think of Pierce?"

"He seems to be a good lawyer, and very pleasant." There was a note of defiance in her voice, challenging him to disagree.

Instead he merely grunted and kept his attention on the trout. "There're dishes in the cabinet to your right, if you wouldn't mind setting the table."

Glad of something to distract herself, she quickly found what she needed and laid them out. Owen took the potatoes from the oven, where he'd had them warming, lightly salted them and quickly sliced a handful of tomatoes. He lifted the trout onto a platter and set it on the table before opening a bottle of white wine.

For an impromptu meal it was both attractive and delicious. "You're a good cook," she said honestly after she had taken her first bite. The trout fairly melted on her tongue.

"Thanks. I ought to be, considering I did it for a living at one time."

"When was that?"

"Back when I was sixteen and out to see the world. I signed on aboard a coal scow out of Aberdeen. That took me as far as Liverpool, and I kept hopping from one berth to another until the wanderlust finally left me several years later." He smiled reminiscingly. "That happened in a bar in Singapore when, strange as it may sound, I suddenly heard these hills calling me and I knew I had to go home."

"What made you leave in the first place?" she asked. The idea of wandering so freely over the earth fascinated her, but it also held an element of fear. She was a better devourer of travel books than she was a traveler herself. Or at least she had always thought so. This trip was turning out to be surprisingly enjoyable.

"Lack of opportunity," he said, refilling their glasses. "Wales has all the usual problems of unemployment, and then some. Many of the young people have to leave."

"But you came back."

"This is my home."

Simple words, but holding a wealth of meaning. He was committed to this place, not only through his labor, but also through his love. He was carving out a niche for himself and he clearly meant to stay.

Which brought home to her the cold reality of her own situation. She was powerfully drawn to a man with whom it would not be possible for her to have any sort of future. They might as well live on separate planets instead of separate continents, so different were their lives.

Sadly she wondered why she couldn't be so attracted to safe, convenient Jeffrey. She was hardly one of those women who only wanted men she couldn't have. But Mother Nature nonetheless seemed intent on thwarting her.

She looked up, finding his eyes on her. In them was a question about limitations and possibilities, and where the one impinged on the other. It was a question she wasn't ready to answer.

Chapter 3

They were still sitting at the table, talking about nothing in particular, when a rumbling to the east distracted them. Gwen looked toward the windows, expecting to see thunderclouds, but instead the darkening sky was clear of all except the first scattering of stars.

The sound came again, deeper and more forcefully than before. The stone floor beneath her feet seemed to vibrate with it. "What . . . ?" she said.

Owen leaned back in his chair, watching her. He had already discovered that he enjoyed doing that. She wasn't just beautiful; there was also an openness about her, and a lack of contrivance, that he found as refreshing as a cool spring on a hot day.

Which made it all the more interesting to see how she would react when he said, "It's the dragon."

She turned startled gray eyes to him. Surely she had heard wrong. "The what?"

"Myrddin's dragon. He's said to live near here. The dragon, not the magician. *His* whereabouts, alas, are unknown."

He sounded so serious—grave, even—that she had to conclude that he wasn't teasing. On the contrary, he might have been discussing any fact about the neighborhood that he apparently presumed she would understand.

"At the risk of sounding like the original dumb bunny," she said, "would you please tell me what you're talking about?"

"You don't know much about Welsh history, do you?"

Owen was evidently given to the indirect reply, a tactic she found more than a little annoying. "I suppose not," she said stiffly. "I do know a fair amount about medieval art, which involves more than a little European history. But British folk tales aren't a specialty."

"Welsh folk tales."

"You're a nationalist."

He was amused by her surprise, but also saddened by it; she was, after all, of Welsh descent. How many generations did a family have to remain in America before the old ties of blood and spirit eroded? He didn't want to believe it could happen so quickly, but perhaps he was wrong.

"Scratch just about any Welshman," he said quietly, "and you'll find one, at least at heart, if not in mind."

"You mean emotionally you'd like to see Wales as a separate country, but rationally you know that isn't possible?"

"That's about the size of it. Though," he added, "I'm sure we both know there are more things possible in this world than anyone would ever suspect."

Gwen had read enough about the nationalist cause to know that its adherents ran the spectrum from a tiny minority of violence-prone extremists to people like Owen, who cherished their Welsh identity and were determined to keep their culture alive.

"All right," she said, "I'll admit to knowing very little about Welsh history. Now, tell me, what has that got to do with dragons?"

"Everything. There used to be a great many of them in Wales. In ancient lore they were one of the three things one does well to hide. I always thought that had a delightfully tongue-in-cheek ring to it, as though anyone could hide a dragon—unless, of course, it was willing. Over in Powys there's a church tower where a dragon was said to spend his nights. In Glamorgan people spoke of winged serpents with iridescent crests of surpassing beauty."

"Perhaps they were some type of animal that survived here long after becoming extinct elsewhere," she ventured, automatically seeking an explanation that would make sense to her modern mind.

He shrugged dismissively. "Or perhaps they weren't creatures of this world at all."

A man who could seriously entertain such a notion was completely outside Gwen's experience. With a hint of desperation she tried to drag the conversation back onto more familiar ground. "So what's all this about Myrddin?"

"You know that's Welsh for Merlin?"

She nodded, glad that her knowledge extended at least that far.

He sat back in his chair to savor the telling of the tale. "Well, it seems that Myrddin was involved in a great deal besides King Arthur and his round table. He was ancient by the time all that happened, near the end of his life, but earlier in his youth he'd had many adventures here in his native Wales."

"All historically documented, of course," she said with unapologetic skepticism.

"Not at all. But, then, the same can be said for the bulk of human experience. It's only been in the last blink of an eye that we've taken to documenting our dubious activities for future generations to wonder at. Back then history was held in memory, passed down from one generation to another in the great sagas and legends."

"Some say myths."

His sapphire eyes narrowed warningly. "And some have no idea how to listen to a story."

"Sorry."

Mollified, he continued. "At any rate, Myrddin was a great man for dragons. He understood them, and they him. It was he who discovered why the stones being used to build King Gwrtheyrn's new capital of Dinas Emyrs persisted in disappearing.

"There was a pool, you see, beneath the building site, and in the pool were two dragons, one white and the other red. Myrddin told the king's men how to find the dragons. When they did, they woke them, and the dragons fought a mighty battle. The white dragon, Myrddin explained, was the champion of the Saxons, while the red dragon fought for the Welsh. Myrddin warned that they would fight on for a very long time until at last the red dragon would triumph. The king took the warning to heart and built his capital elsewhere, but forever after the red dragon has been the symbol of Wales."

He smiled entrancingly. "You see him everywhere, including on the Welsh flag, but when's the last time you saw a white dragon?"

"You've got me," Gwen admitted. She was feeling pleasantly bemused, as though she had wandered into some marvelous dream where everything had its own reality.

"At any rate," he continued, "to get back to your original question, Myrddin was acquainted with many dragons. He knew their habits and their hiding places. It's long been believed that one of them lived in a cave not far from here and that every once in a while he still makes his presence known."

"I don't suppose," she ventured, "that you'd buy the idea that the rumbling we heard could have been caused by a fault in the earth, some sort of geological phenomenon, that sort of thing?"

Owen appeared to consider that for a moment, but shook his head. "I don't see how that makes any more sense than a dragon in a cave."

"No, I guess you wouldn't. Where is this alleged cave?"

"Under your house."

"What?"

"Beneath Myrddin's Rock, toward the sea."

"You're telling me that I'm living on top of an insomniac dragon?"

"If it's any consolation, he's supposed to bring good fortune to the owner of Myrddin's Rock."

"I can just see the ad now," Gwen said, rolling her eyes. "'For Sale, picturesque Welsh castle—complete with benevolent dragon.' That should bring in the offers."

Owen's smile had faded. In its place was watchfulness. "So you're still determined to sell?"

She glanced away uncomfortably. "I don't see that I have any choice."

"Because your life is in America?"

"Don't you think that's a good enough reason?"

"I suppose."

He had surprised her. She had expected further argument and was almost disappointed that he didn't seem willing to pursue the subject. Instead he asked, "How much longer are you planning to stay?"

"A few weeks. I have some vacation time saved up."

"Then perhaps you'll let me show you around."

It seemed she wasn't going to lack for company. But if Daniel Pierce was a safely pleasant tour guide, Owen was a very different matter. Every moment she spent in his presence made her more vividly aware of the dangerous yet enthralling currents moving between them. A small frisson of excitement coursed through her as she looked at him. Eccentric he might be, but in the most delightful way.

"You could show me the dragon cave," she suggested, only half-facetiously.

"Or at least we could search for it. How about a picnic tomorrow?"

"I'd like that, but I promised—" She broke off, having never been the sort to dangle one man in front of another.

In this case she didn't have to. Owen got the message and promptly scowled. "Don't expect Pierce to go looking for dragons."

The mere thought of that made her laugh, which defused Owen's annoyance. He grinned despite himself. "I've nothing against him personally, you know. It's only that we don't agree on much."

She could well believe it. The two men were as different as night and day. Owen was dark, mysterious, not truly part of the mundane world, whereas Daniel seemed perfectly straightforward, open and accessible, part of the life she understood and was comfortable with.

Which failed to explain why she had a sudden yen to go dragon hunting.

"We can do it the next day," Owen suggested, watching her.

She agreed readily enough even as a tiny voice of caution whispered in the back of her mind that it really wasn't prudent to see too much of him. Surely there could be no harm in a single afternoon spent together searching for a wakeful dragon.

Owen insisted on walking her back to what, over dinner, they had teasingly begun to refer to as "the castle." Time had passed without her awareness, and it had come on full night before she realized the lateness of the hour. Lacking a moon, the darkness was Stygian. She would have been hard-pressed to find her hand in front of her face.

Owen, conversely, had no difficulty finding his way, but in deference to her city-dulled sensibilities he fetched a flashlight from a cabinet and used it to shine a thin beam along the road.

As they left the house something large and swift moved into position beside them. Gwen, taken by surprise, let out a soft exclamation and backed away.

"It's all right," Owen said reassuringly as he bent down to scratch the creature's ears. "This is Lancelot. He's harmless, though he likes to think otherwise."

Judging by the slightly manic look in Lancelot's eyes, she could well believe it. Closer examination revealed him to be a Welsh sheepdog, one of the breed that patrolled the nooks and crannies of endless hillsides in search of strays from the flocks. Besides those intent brown eyes staring at her, he was the proud possessor of a lolling tongue, a wagging tail and a body that was positively quivering with delight. Apparently her mere existence was enough to send him into ecstasies.

"He's, uh, very enthusiastic," she said as the dog lovingly licked her hand and then started on her arm.

Owen pulled him away with a grin. "You could say he has good taste."

"More like I taste good to him."

Lancelot looked brightly from one to the other of them and appeared to smile his agreement. As they began to move through the darkness he kept close to their side.

Just as her eyes had trouble adjusting, so did Gwen's ears. At first she thought what she heard was silence, until she listened more closely and began to pick out the rhythmic night sounds of myriad creatures. The hum of insects, the soft hooting of owls and the sporadic rustlings off in the shadows made her aware of all the life going on around them. Lancelot growled at something nearby, but made no effort to run after it.

The night air was fragrant with the scents of damp earth and flowering gorse; of cattle and hay; of dew ponds slumbering under algae, and twisted oaks softened by communities of lichen; and always of the sea, never more than a murmuring breeze away.

They passed through an old iron gate that Owen held open for her. It creaked plaintively, as though offended at being required to move at such a late hour.

"There was a farm here not too many years ago," Owen said, his voice muted in the darkness. "A family named Jones had it. But the sons grew up and left for greener pastures. After a while it became too much for the parents to manage and they sold out."

"It's unfortunate how often that happens, even in the States."

"I've heard about the farm problem there," he said, "and I agree it's bad. But here we're dealing with people who have often worked the same land not for three or four generations but for centuries. When they have to leave they might as well be cutting out their hearts."

"I suppose they go to the cities," she said quietly.

"And try to find work, often without success. Things aren't much better there."

"There has to be a solution. More industrialization, perhaps."

"Have you seen what the coal mines did to Wales?"

"No," she admitted, "but I've seen strip mining in West Virginia, and it wasn't pretty."

"Neither is this. The land has been raped and brutalized until it's a wonder that it's survived at all."

He spoke with a cold note of rage that did not completely mask his aching sorrow. Gwen was struck by the depth of his feeling. Hers had been an urban upbringing in which there was little contact with nature or the land. She was capable of appreciating a pretty bit of scenery, but that was about all.

Yet she could feel deep within herself a sense of something far more, of true communion with a particular part of the earth that was not mere soil and rock, but an actual living presence.

So struck was she by what that must actually be like that she failed to pay proper attention to the road and stumbled. Owen's arm lashed out to catch her. She bit back a gasp as their bodies came into contact.

"Easy," he murmured thickly. "You have to be more careful."

Wise words, even if she could barely comprehend them. All her senses were engulfed by the storm of feelings coursing through her. She knew only the steely strength of his arm wrapped around her waist, the rock hardness of his chest against which her breasts rested, the sheer masculine power of him, in such sharp contrast to her own femininity.

A femininity of which she had never before been so acutely aware. They were alone, a man and a woman, in a velvet night turned incandescent by the desire coursing between them like a fast-moving flow of lava shot from the earth's core.

Owen breathed in sharply, taking the scent of her—lemon and musk, and pure woman—into the very essence of his being. Distantly he wondered at what was happening to him. He had known sexual hunger before, even lust, but never anything that resembled the forces at work between them.

It was as though every part of his body and soul were reaching out to her, as a man dying of thirst might strain toward a crystalline pool. His need for her was no mere sensual indulgence, but a craving as fundamental as that for life itself.

All of which disturbed him greatly. Because he was a man who understood at least something of the tremendous powers of nature, he was also respectfully leery of them. And he was conscious of his own vulnerability. He didn't need a relationship with a woman who would only leave him hurting.

And yet there was the tantalizing softness of her body pressed against him, the silken temptation of her glistening hair, the sweet invitation of her lips parted on a soft gasp.

Slowly he bent his head. Wanting to pull back, yet unable to do so, he touched his mouth to hers. Only a kiss, he told himself, nothing more. Enough to satisfy his curiosity about her and convince him that she was no different from other, safer women he could amuse himself with.

He was lying. She was different because—and this truly frightened him—he recognized her. The feel of her mouth beneath his was familiar in the same way as the first sight of a man's home after a long absence strums chords of memory, except that in this case that wasn't possible.

He had seen her for the first time the day before, had never even heard her name until a few months before Winny's death, when she mentioned who would be getting the house.

They had talked for a long time then, until afternoon faded into night. He could still hear his old friend's soft voice rising and falling as she explained her wishes and her hopes.

When he had promised to do everything possible to see that they came true, he had meant it. But it hadn't occurred to him how high the price might be.

Gwen was all warm sweetness and yielding beguilement. Her mouth was fragrant, and when he touched his tongue to the ridge of her teeth, she moaned softly. His arms tightened around her. Driven by the need to let her feel the full force of his hunger, he plunged more deeply.

She met him with equal fierceness. There was no holding back, no coy display of reluctance, only honest need, enticing in its starkness.

And terrifying. Gwen had never felt anything remotely like this. Secretly, in the most private part of her mind, she had sometimes wondered a little at her lack of ardor. However much she might aesthetically appreciate a man, even like him and want to know him better, she had never experienced the heady desire that was the stuff of poetry and a certain kind of novel. If the truth were told, she had doubted that it existed.

Now she knew better. It was as though all her restraint, all her inhibitions, all her natural caution, had vanished in an instant. There was nothing left except the two of them, the night and the glittering promise of what they could share.

If they'd had only minutes together, they might have put them to the best possible use. What prevented them was the shared knowledge that they had time. Not much, but some.

She had said she would stay for several weeks, and she still meant to, if only to discover whether what they experienced on the night-darkened road could also exist in the bright light of day.

Chapter 4

After Owen left her at her door, Gwen took a hot bath, treated herself to a brandy and otherwise did her best to relax. It had cooled off considerably from earlier in the day, and she was glad of the bedroom fireplace, in which she lit several blocks of the peat that had been stored in a wooden chest nearby. Peat burned far more quietly and slowly than wood, and scented the room with a distinctive homey odor that was oddly comforting.

Curled up in bed, she read for a while from the works of Thomas Malory, which she had found in the sitting room. It had been several years since she had last delved into the stories of King Arthur and his round table, and her mind was soon filled once again with visions of heroic struggle and a Utopian kingdom ultimately brought down by deceit and human frailty.

She went to bed a little later than usual in the hope of falling asleep promptly, only to discover that it was not to be.

Lying awake in the four-poster, she stared at the remnants of the fire and tried not to think about what had happened on the road. She might as well have tried to stop breathing. Irresistible images of Owen, and of her with him, rose to taunt her.

"Gwen, my girl," she finally murmured under her breath, "it's getting time to fish or cut bait."

How would it hurt to have one glorious, stupendous affair? Something to chuckle over when she was an old lady, perhaps even something to shock her children with, though using only the most veiled allusions, of course. She could get Owen out of her system, go home, marry Jeffrey and settle down. Not a bad plan at all.

Or it would have been if she hadn't been burdened by scruples. She would be using Owen, and using herself, taking advantage of their hunger for each other in a way that simply didn't seem right.

Glumly she turned over on her side, her cheek pillowed on her hand. "I can just hear him now. 'Go ahead, take advantage.' Any red-blooded male would say the same."

Which was certainly what he was, no doubt about that. She shivered as she remembered the strength of his hands on her, the skill of his mouth, the power of his long, hard body. The silk nightgown she wore moved sensuously over her skin as she turned over.

She closed her eyes against the wave of anticipatory sensation as she imagined Owen removing it from her. Instinct told her that he would be a magnificent lover, tender but demanding, patient but insistent. She didn't doubt that she could reach the pinnacle of pleasure with him. But then what?

"Your problem," she told herself, "is that you're a romantic. That doesn't work in this world."

Didn't she, after all, know numerous people who had long since put aside whatever fantasies they had about love and commitment and settled for a series of relationships that were physically satisfying, at least?

They had given up expecting anything more of life and seemed content enough with what they did have, whereas she was always looking for the next rainbow, the next dragon beating iridescent wings across a midnight sky.

"Grow up," she muttered. "Owen is an attractive man. He makes your toes curl and your insides melt. So go to bed with him. Honestly, he won't hold it against you."

At least he wouldn't if he was like the general run of the men she knew. But something warned her that he was different. He cared, for one thing, about issues others preferred to ignore. He wasn't afraid to put himself on the line emotionally, at least, not where his beloved Wales was concerned. He didn't play it safe, hiding behind button-down collars and plastic smiles.

Like Daniel? That wasn't fair. She barely knew the lawyer and was in no position to be making judgments about him beyond his obvious professional capabilities. It was hardly Daniel's fault that he wasn't as virilely handsome, as compellingly fascinating, as Owen.

She sighed deeply and turned over onto her back, seeking a more comfortable position without success. The mattress was pleasantly firm, the sheets smooth and cool, the room lightly scented with peat and salt air. She should have been sleeping soundly, and she would have been, if every time she closed her eyes she hadn't seen a half mocking, half enticing sapphire gaze.

"Damn him," she muttered, rising at last in frustration. This was getting her nowhere. She got out of bed, walked carefully down the curving stairs and made her way to the kitchen.

She had left a light on, and it cast a cheerful glow over the old-fashioned room. Seated at the worn wood table with a glass of milk, she stared out the window until she caught herself thinking how nice fresh curtains would look.

As well as Winny had kept the place, it was clear that in the last years of her life she had felt little enthusiasm for making changes. She had been an elderly lady, content to live surrounded by familiar things, so long as they were clean and tidy.

Her taste must have been very much like Gwen's, because there was little she would change, except for the curtains and perhaps a new rug in the bedroom. Thicker towels in bright colors would be nice, too, and...

"Stop that," she reprimanded herself. "You're leaving here in a few weeks, and you'll never see the place again. Stop pretending it's home."

Home was the apartment in Cambridge; the pleasant, orderly life she had made for herself; her work and her friends. It was not a castle perched on top of a dragon's lair, facing the sea.

She finished the milk, rinsed out the glass and set it on the drainboard. Despite her best efforts she felt no sleepier than she had before. Tired, certainly, but not capable of sleep.

Nonetheless she started up the stone steps again, determined to get at least some rest. She was halfway up when the same rumbling she had heard at Owen's came again, only this time it was clearly much closer at hand.

Gwen gasped as she automatically reached out to steady herself. The stairs had no banister, and the smooth, cool stone walls gave her nothing to hold on to. Deep and ominous, like summer thunder that seems to roll clear across the sky, the rumbling continued. She could feel it beneath her feet, its vibrations reaching up through her very bones.

It had to be an earth tremor. No other explanation made any sense, no matter what Owen said. But somehow that didn't seem to calm her fears. She pressed herself against the stone wall and squeezed her eyes tightly shut. She didn't open them again until the sound at last died away.

Even then she didn't move at once, but waited until her heartbeat returned to some semblance of normality before attempting the rest of the stairs. White-faced and trembling, she finally reached the bedroom and dropped onto the bed, clutching fistfuls of the covers as though to anchor herself.

Definitely an earth tremor. Myrddin's Rock must have been built directly on top of an ancient fault line. With a wan laugh she wondered at the stubbornness of her ancestors who had insisted on remaining in such a place.

Oddly that thought cheered her, and she was able to lie back. "Go to sleep, dragon," she murmured even as her eyes fluttered shut.

The phone was still out when she checked it early the next morning. Though she had ended up sleeping surprisingly well, she had still awakened shortly after dawn, in time to see the lawns around the castle glistening with webs of dew.

She smiled as she remembered her father telling her that the fairies spun the webs to collect the dew, with which they bathed their wings to make them shine.

Images of fairy folk cavorting in the early-morning light stayed with her as she showered and dressed, then went downstairs to fix breakfast. But first she tried the phone again, only to discover that she was still cut off.

She and Daniel hadn't set a time to meet, so she had presumed he would call. But Owen had indicated that phone problems weren't unusual, so it was likely Daniel would simply come by.

On the chance that he would be early she made a full pot of coffee and was just sitting down to her first cup, when she heard footsteps on the gravel path leading to the kitchen door.

Rising, she glanced out the window in time to see Owen approaching, with Lancelot at his heels.

"Good morning," she said, opening the door to him. If possible he looked even more appealing than he had the night before. Each time she encountered him, she seemed to see more, as though contact with him heightened her perception and gave her the ability to look beyond the superficial.

For instance, she no longer saw simply a man whom nature had happened to gift with a devastatingly attractive face and body. Rather she saw beyond, to the essence of his strength, and to something else she couldn't identify that was still partially hidden from her.

All she was certain of was that he was troubled, and not for the reasons he chose to state.

"I was worried about you," he said. "There was another tremor last night."

"Yes, I felt it. Does anyone take seismographic readings around here? They could keep very busy."

He cast her a swift, impenetrable glance as he slipped into a chair. As she poured him a mug of coffee, leaving it black as she had already noticed he liked, he said, "No one takes much of an interest."

"Why not? There's clearly a fault line around here. It's a wonder there hasn't been a major earthquake."

"Oh, I don't think there's any danger of that." He tilted his chair on its rear legs, regarding her steadily. She was aware of how easily he managed his body, with none of the clumsiness so large a man might have shown. He was graceful and agile, almost as though at some point in his life he had undergone extensive physical training, though for what purpose she couldn't imagine.

"Local records go back almost a thousand years," he continued, "and don't mention anything of that sort. Besides, I told you, it's the dragon."

His insistence on that facetious explanation obscurely annoyed her. "Have it your way," she said. "There was no harm done, so your concern wasn't necessary."

His square jaw stiffened slightly, but he said only, "I'm glad to hear you weren't frightened."

Reluctantly she said, "Actually, I was, for a few moments. It seemed as though it would never end."

His face softened, though many people might not have noticed the change. She was already becoming so well attuned to the slightest nuances of his expression that she could recognize the swift flashes of gentleness that illuminated it. "There's nothing to be frightened of. You wouldn't have been hurt."

"I was on the stairs at the time. The way everything seemed to be moving, I could have fallen."

A veil dropped over his eyes. "You felt movement?"

"Not exactly. I felt the sound. It reached straight through me."

"Then you'll probably have a hard time believing me when I tell you that most people never feel it, or, for that matter, hear it."

"That's impossible," she said flatly. Earth tremors were hardly selective in their audience.

"I know," Owen admitted. "But it still happens. Winny could feel it, and she told me her father also had the ability. But people from the village who happen to be nearby when it occurs aren't generally aware of anything."

"But you felt it," she protested.

He was silent for a moment, then nodded slowly. "Yes, I know."

They were still staring at each other when Lancelot, who had settled at Owen's feet, woofed a soft warning. "Easy, boy," Owen said, laying a hand on the dog's head. Gwen rose, already knowing who she would find at the door this time.

"Come in, Daniel," she said after greeting the lawyer. "I suppose you know the phone is out?"

"Yes, I tried to reach you but—" He stopped in midsentence, taking in the big man stretched out comfortably at the kitchen table.

"Morning, Pierce," Owen said with an amiable smile.

Gwen was suddenly aware of how the scene must look. Owen was very much at his ease, with his hair rumpled and his shirt partly undone. There were two cups of coffee on the table, and the makings for breakfast were laid out nearby. At such an early hour anyone could be excused for thinking he had spent the night.

"Owen just dropped by," she hastened to explain, ignoring his amused look, "to make sure there hadn't been any damage from the earth tremor."

"The what?" Daniel asked, still looking at the other man.

Gwen turned back to him with the coffeepot in her hand. "You didn't feel anything?"

"I don't know what you're referring to." With an effort he wrenched his attention away from Owen and turned it to her. "We don't have earth tremors around here."

Despite herself, Gwen's gaze flew to Owen, who was smiling smugly. She returned a scowl. "Never mind. Why don't you sit down? I was just going to do something about breakfast."

"I wouldn't want to intrude," Daniel said stiffly.

"But I thought we were going sight-seeing?"

"I'm the one who's in the way," Owen said cheerfully, rising to his feet. "Thanks for the coffee, Gwen. Let me know about tomorrow."

"Oh, yes, certainly." She went with him to the door, silently beseeching him to stop grinning. He didn't, nor did he hesitate to drop a light but provocative kiss on her upturned mouth before raising a blithe hand to Daniel and disappearing down the path, Lancelot at his heels.

"Cheeky fellow," Daniel muttered as soon as he was gone. "No manners."

"He seems nice enough," she murmured as she closed the door behind him.

"Don't let him fool you. No one around here knows much about him, despite the fact that he's owned that old wreck of a place some five years now. He's close-mouthed, stays to himself and is away regularly for weeks at a time."

"Those are hardly crimes," Gwen said noncommittally, though she was interested in the bit about Owen going away. Clearly his life was not as settled as he had led her to believe.

"If you'll forgive me for saying so, you seem like a very trusting sort of person."

Gwen turned away to hide her amusement. She supposed that he was right, up to a point, but she doubted that he had any idea how adept a woman living alone in a big city got at taking care of herself.

"Are you warning me that I shouldn't be, Daniel?"

"All I'm saying is that it's wiser to be more... cautious around certain people."

She returned to the table with a plate of warm scones and a bowl of honey. "I take it you don't include yourself?"

He flushed and looked taken aback. "Of course not. It was Owen I was referring to. You're a . . . very attractive woman, and, to be blunt about it, he has a certain reputation."

So far, to the best of Gwen's recollection, Daniel had attempted to cast Owen in the role of indigent ne'er-do-well, sinister stranger and now, it seemed, reprobate. She wondered at the source of the enmity between them as she split a scone and dribbled honey on it.

"Really," she said. "I would have thought that any man who lives in a monastery . . ."

"Surely you're not fooled by that!" he exclaimed. "There haven't been monks there in centuries."

"Yet there's still a certain air about the place."

Daniel might not be as quick on the uptake as he should be, but he wasn't hopelessly dense, either. The implication of what she said finally sank in.

"You've been over there," he said.

She nodded. "Yesterday, when I found that the phone was out. I thought I might be able to use Owen's to call for service, but his wasn't working, either."

"But you saw the way he lives." Recovering something of his equanimity, Daniel asked, "What do you think of it?"

"It's fascinating. Have a scone."

He accepted one, along with a cup of coffee, while waiting for her to elaborate. "The restoration he's done so far is authentic, yet practical. He seems to have achieved a nice blend between the past and the present."

"But what good is it, besides sheer self-indulgence? It's the future of Wales we have to be concerned with."

Gwen could understand that view, even if she didn't agree with it. Gently she said, "Surely the future has to be built on what went before."

"Only if that happens to be worth saving. In our case, I'm afraid it isn't."

"That's a very harsh judgment to make." So much so that she was taken aback by it. By inclination as well as by training, she treasured the past. While she understood that many people gave it scant thought, the idea of wanting to jettison it entirely horrified her.

"What is there to save," Daniel demanded, "except a legacy of poverty and defeat? Do you have any idea how many times Wales has been conquered? How many rebellions have failed? How many people have lived and died in misery simply because they didn't have the sense to accept the reality of their situation, preferring the dream of a mythical past that made us our own worst enemies?"

His harsh vehemence puzzled her. Until that moment he had seemed mild mannered, even emotionless. But clearly that was not the case. A broad streak of anger lurked beneath his seemingly calm exterior.

"Daniel, there are things in any people's past that they would rather had been different. That doesn't mean they have anything to be ashamed of."

"Easy for you to say. You're an American. You come from a country accustomed to power and wealth. You have no idea what it's like to have your face ground into the dirt century after century."

"We've had our share of problems," Gwen insisted quietly. "The Civil War almost tore America apart. So did what happened in Vietnam. We've gone through long periods of self-doubt."

"It's not the same thing," he insisted. "You've never been conquered, never had your homes and lands seized by a victorious enemy, never had everything you hold dear abused and destroyed. You have no idea what it is to feel totally helpless, unable even to protect your women and children. That's the legacy Wales draws from the past. It festers in us and weakens our resolve to work for the future."

She could hardly deny that, as an American, she had no experience with what he was describing. But neither could she accept the idea that the past could ever be regarded as useless. "Surely we learn from what's gone before us?"

He cast her a quick, sharp look. "You'd think so, wouldn't you? But some people never do. They go on making the same mistakes, enduring the same sorrows, all because they lack any confidence in their ability to effect change."

"You don't."

"What do you mean?"

"Lack confidence. I don't think you would speak as you do about change unless you were absolutely convinced it was going to happen."

"I suppose that's true," he acknowledged. "At least, I'm fully committed to it."

Just as Owen was committed to the preservation of the past. The two men had something in common, after all, though their dedication took very different forms.

As though aware that the conversation had veered onto more serious ground than he wished, Daniel smiled apologetically. "I promised you a tour, not a lecture."

"I don't mind," Gwen assured him. On the contrary, she found what he had to say interesting, if disturbing.

Nonetheless Daniel insisted that they make a start. He seemed eager to show her around Castell Myrddin and the surrounding area.

"The village dates from at least the twelfth century," he explained when they were seated in his aged but well-cared-for Aston Martin. "It was about then that the English started taking a strong interest in Wales, the descendants of William the Conqueror being as rapacious as their illustrious forebears. Down through the years, the various royal dynasties—Plantagenet, Tudor, Stuart and so on—have awarded the land to various families that happened to merit royal favor. But there's strong reason to believe that this entire area once belonged to your own people."

"The Llywelyns? I presumed they'd been here a while because of Winny's castle, but I had no idea they'd owned all the land."

"Owned isn't exactly right," Daniel said. "They were clan chieftains, chosen for their superior abilities as leaders. Celtic people were much more democratic in their approach to government than the Normans who came after them."

"For a man who discounts history," Gwen said, "you aren't ignorant of it."

He shot her a look she couldn't decipher. "I've always believed it's wise to know the enemy."

She was still chewing over what he meant by that when they entered the village. Daniel pointed out the parish church as they passed, and Gwen decided to pay a visit to Winny's grave.

"Is there someplace I could buy flowers?" she asked.

"Mrs. Gascoigne usually has some at the grocery store." He parked the car and helped her out, and together they strolled down the narrow main street. Once again Gwen was subjected to the surreptitious looks of passersby, who nodded politely to Daniel.

Amused, she asked, "How long would I have to live here before being accepted by the locals?"

"You're not thinking of staying?"

She shook her head. "I just wondered."

"Ordinarily I'd have to say that because you weren't born here, you'd never be fully accepted. Anglesey is a very insulated place, and Castell Myrddin even more so. But since you're Winny's grandniece, you might eventually acquire at least a veneer of belonging."

"You seem to be fully accepted."

"Oh, I was born here," he explained. "Before I went away to school I knew every nook and cranny of these hills."

"Then perhaps you've met the dragon," she said with a smile as they entered the store. It was small and cluttered, and smelled of sawdust and ripe cheese. There were the usual stacks of cans and boxes. A small display case held a few forlorn cartons of ice cream and a single frozen pie, and behind the counter was a pegboard on which hung brooms and brushes of every description.

The personage ruling over all this was so small that at first Gwen thought she was looking at a child, except that no child would have a face so wizened or eyes so wise.

"Good morning to you, Daniel," the tiny old woman in a faded paisley dress said. "And to you, Miss."

"Mrs. Gascoigne," Daniel said respectfully, "this is Gwen Llywelyn, Winny's great-niece."

Gwen was sure that it was only simple courtesy that prevented the proprietress from admitting to a prior knowledge of her identity. Certainly little could be expected to escape the scrutiny of those sharp black eyes, especially not the presence of a stranger in the village. As Mrs. Gascoigne looked her over, she had the uncomfortable feeling that the old woman was seeing far beyond the surface.

"A pleasure to meet you, dear," she said in a high frail voice that nonetheless rang with self-assurance. "Winny and I were friends going way back. I miss her."

Those simple words brought an unexpected lump to Gwen's throat. Living in her great-aunt's home, among all her things, she felt a strange but pleasant communion with the dead woman that made her wish she had known her in life. That was impossible, but at least she could become acquainted with those who had cared about her.

"I'm happy to meet you, Mrs. Gascoigne. I only wish I could have come here sooner, while Winny was still alive."

"Well, dear, these things tend to work out for the best. Now, then, is there something I can get for you?"

Gwen asked if there were any flowers for sale, and Mrs. Gascoigne showed her to a sunny corner of the store, where several metal containers held an assortment of freshly cut roses, daisies and irises.

"Most people around here grow their own," she said, "but occasionally someone likes to pick a pretty bouquet."

Gwen made her selection and returned to the counter. Daniel was glancing through a rack of magazines, but turned when she approached. "All set?" he asked.

She nodded, waiting as Mrs. Gascoigne rang up her purchase on an old, ornately gilded cash register.

Picking up a weekly business magazine, he said casually, "By the way, what was that you were saying about a dragon?"

Mrs. Gascoigne's gnarled fingers paused on the cash register keys.

"Dragon?" Gwen repeated. "Oh, I was asking if you'd met him. Owen says he lives in a cave under Myrddin's Rock."

Daniel grimaced and ran a hand through his straight blond hair. "Owen would say something like that. More nonsense."

"Don't be sure of that, laddie," Mrs. Gascoigne murmured. "There are stranger things under this sun than you or I will ever know."

"I must admit," Gwen said, "that I rather like the idea of a world in which there are still dragons."

The old woman and Daniel exchanged a glance. Mrs. Gascoigne's withered face softened. "Believe whatever you wish, dear. Don't ever let anyone take your dreams from you."

"Oh, I wasn't really serious," Gwen said hastily, not wanting to give the wrong impression. "Just fanciful."

Mrs. Gascoigne shrugged. "Fancy is as fancy does. Winny was very fond of dragons."

"Was she?" Gwen asked, interested despite herself. The conversation had a tenor of unreality that was oddly reassuring.

"She thought them splendid creatures, though they can be dangerous."

Daniel murmured something under his breath, which drew Mrs. Gascoigne's attention to him. "I know well enough what you think of such things, Daniel Pierce. But you're young yet, and when you've gotten a few more years on you, perhaps you'll learn you aren't quite as smart as you think you are."

"Now, Mrs. Gascoigne," he said with a smile, "don't be painting me a callow boy in front of Miss Llywelyn."

The sharp black eyes looked back and forth from him to Gwen. "Is that the way of it, then? Well, I won't say another word. Only take these flowers, dear," she said, handing the bouquet to Gwen, "and give Winny my best."

"I didn't tell her why I wanted the flowers," Gwen said after they had left the store and were once more back on the street. They had to pause a moment to let their eyes adjust to the brightness, which was almost dazzling after the shadows inside.

"It was a reasonable guess," Daniel said. "Don't let that old lady fool you. She puts on a fine, mystical air, but at heart she's as practical as they come."

"Was she really Winny's friend?"

"Oh, yes," he assured her. "Most of the older people around here were. They all grew up together, you see. And there was a special bond."

"Based on what?" Gwen asked as they walked down the street toward the churchyard.

"It's hard to explain exactly, but the Llywelyns, being such an old family in these parts, always took an interest in the general welfare. People could go to Winny with their problems and she'd do her best to help them."

"It sounds as though she were some sort of lady of the manor."

"Not exactly, because she never thought she was superior to anyone else, but it's true that she felt a special sense of responsibility."

Which she had inherited, Gwen thought, as surely as she had inherited Myrddin's Rock. Except that she was selling out.

"Do you still think you'll have no trouble finding a buyer?" she asked Daniel.

"Not given a bit of time. I'll have those papers drawn up for you to sign this week."

Gwen nodded, despite the surge of doubt that moved through her. Of course she was doing the right thing. It made perfect sense to sell. But as she knelt beside the still fresh soil covering her great-aunt's grave and gently laid the flowers on it, she couldn't help thinking that she was on the verge of betraying a trust she hadn't even come close to understanding.

Chapter 5

The dragon was quiet that night. Gwen slept well. She suspected on awakening that she had dreamed of Owen, but she couldn't remember clearly.

She had spent a pleasant day with Daniel, seeing the village and the countryside. Anglesey was an undeniably lovely place, rugged and beautiful at the same time. Her enjoyment had been only slightly spoiled by her guide's insistence on describing how the land and its resources were being wasted.

"There's no capital," Daniel explained. "That's the problem. No one wants to invest here, despite the fact that so much could be done. High-tech factories, for instance, assembling microchips or entire computers. Fish-processing plants, mining, there's no end to the possibilities."

"I understand what you're saying," Gwen told him. "People need work, and industry would bring wealth into the area. But from what I can see there's already a good way of life here. Not luxurious, but solid and stable. What's so wrong about that?"

"It's not going anywhere," Daniel insisted. "People live virtually the same way they have for generations. There's no progress. Without that we remain powerless, and you already know what I think of that."

Gwen really hadn't wanted to get him started on that again, so she refrained from further comment. He seemed to understand her disinclination and changed the subject.

The rest of the day passed enjoyably, as did the dinner they shared at a small inn nestled away in the countryside. She returned home tired but refreshed.

A smile flitted across her face as she turned on the water to fill the tub the next morning, reflecting that she had discovered yet another difference between Owen and Daniel. Owen had not hesitated to make his interest in her clear. Daniel, on the other hand, was far more restrained. He had made no effort to kiss her, let alone go any further.

As she lay in the water she laughed as she reminded herself that he simply might not be attracted to her. She was hardly a femme fatale who swept men off their feet. Yet he had gone out of his way to spend time with her, more than could be expected from a conscientious attorney being polite to a client.

The pipes rattled suddenly, and the flow of water stopped abruptly. Gwen stood looking at the faucet for a moment before realizing that whatever the problem might be, it wasn't going to miraculously correct itself.

Grumbling, she got out of the tub and toweled herself dry, glad that she had at least gotten the soap out of her hair before the water stopped.

Charming though Myrddin's Rock might be, the house needed a lot of work. The longer she stayed, the more she realized that. At least the phone was functioning again. She had checked the dial tone on her way into the kitchen.

The refrigerator was beginning to look empty. She needed to shop, but she had also arranged to spend the day with Owen. When he hadn't shown up by the time she finished breakfast, she wondered if he had forgotten.

She tried to call him, but his line was busy, and after a few minutes' hesitation she decided to walk over to his place. The day was sunny and pleasant, with the ever present sea breeze keeping the air from becoming too warm.

Sheep grazed on the hillsides, and off in the distance she could hear the barking of dogs rounding up the next lot to be sheared. From the path that skirted the sea she caught sight of a fishing boat and waved to the distant men, who returned her greeting.

Lancelot bounded out to welcome her as she came down the path toward the old monastery. He wagged his tail and lavished several licks on her hand. Laughing, she bent and scratched him behind the ears, eliciting even more frantic appreciation.

"You're just ferocious, aren't you?" she crooned as his eyes rolled ecstatically. "Nobody messes with you, do they, boy?" He rolled over, his paws in the air, and let her tickle his belly.

"Much more of that," Owen said, "and he'll fly completely apart. We'll have bits of goofy dog all over the place."

Gwen got to her feet as Lancelot threw himself eagerly at his master. She brushed her hands off as she studied him. He looked tired; there were faint shadows beneath his eyes, and the lines on either side of his firm mouth were more pronounced than usual.

"Are you busy?" she asked.

"Not particularly. Besides, isn't this my day to show you around?"

She flushed slightly, hoping that he couldn't sense her eagerness. "If it's no trouble."

He laughed softly. "None at all. Come in for a moment while I pick up what we need, then we'll be on our way."

The great stone-walled kitchen was tidy, except for a newspaper unfolded on the table. Gwen glanced at it in passing, only to stop when she noticed the headline.

"What's that about a bombing?" she asked.

He had his back to her as he finished whatever he'd been doing. "In Cardiff, last night. Prince Charles is scheduled to make a visit there soon, and it looks as though someone was planning a little surprise for him. Only they got one themselves when whatever they were working on exploded prematurely."

"How awful," Gwen murmured. "I'll never be able to understand that kind of mentality," she said. "How can anyone justify murder?"

Owen shrugged as he turned back to her. "Terrorists come in all sorts of guises, but they all have one thing in common—complete amorality. They can excuse any action so long as it suits their purposes."

Though he spoke quietly enough, there was an underlying note of anger in his voice that surprised Gwen. He almost seemed to take the situation personally.

Before she could pursue that thought any further, he smiled suddenly and said, "I hope a picnic appeals to you?"

She noticed then the basket that he held in one hand. It looked large enough to hold a meal for half a dozen hungry stevedores, let alone two sight-seers. "Sure," she said with a grin. "Provided we've got enough to eat."

"I think I can promise that," he said as they left the house. Lancelot followed, but stood at attention at the start of the flagstone path.

"Guard, boy," Owen said.

The dog appeared to nod. He took up his post by the door, clearly prepared to stay there no matter what.

Around the back of the blacksmith shed, a battered Jeep was parked. Gwen took one look at it and her eyes widened. "I won't even ask how many miles you've got on this thing."

"Good," he said as he helped her into it. "Because I've got no idea. The odometer stopped working several years ago."

"Probably wouldn't go any higher," she murmured as she tried to get comfortable in what felt literally like a bucket seat.

"Gets great mileage," Owen said complacently as he slid behind the wheel. "I picked it up from a retired sergeant major who had fought with Montgomery at Tobruk."

"In this very vehicle, I presume."

"Well . . . he never actually told me that."

Their laughter was sweet on the morning air. Owen took the road that led along the shore. Sea gulls whirled overhead, and sunlight shimmered on the foam-crested water. Gwen was content to sit in silence, drinking in the beauty surrounding them.

When Owen pulled the Jeep off to the side of the road she was almost disappointed until he pointed to a narrow path cutting through the underbrush. "Are you game to follow that?" he asked.

"Of course. Where does it lead?"

"Eventually to the beach beneath Myrddin's Rock, but it's a bit of a hike."

"Does that mean you carry the picnic basket?" she teased.

He assured her that it did, and they set off, Owen going first with the basket, and Gwen following with the blanket he had taken from the back seat. The way down was steep, and she was glad of his steadying presence directly ahead of her.

"Careful," he said when they had gone a short distance. "There are loose stones here. You could turn your ankle."

She took the warning to heart and watched where she stepped, though the temptation to look at the scenery was all but irresistible.

Before them lay a beach of golden sand studded with boulders on which lichen had painted myriad colors. It looked like a giant's playground, where humans could only venture cautiously.

Over the next rise she caught sight of Myrddin's Rock, its tower framed against the cloudless sky. A rush of pride washed over her as she thought of the generations of Llywelyns who had contemplated the same scene.

Hard on it came the reminder that she would be the last to do so. She blinked sharply against the sudden sting of tears, which she told herself was caused by the sharpness of the breeze.

The path continued downward, and a short time later they reached the beach. Above them the cliff loomed; ahead lay the sea. They were the only two people in sight; the only sounds were the raucous gulls and the ebb and flow of the waves.

"The tide is out," Owen said as he set the basket down, "so it's safe to be here. But you should keep in mind that at high tide the beach is completely covered and the path can be hard to find."

"I don't plan on coming here alone," Gwen assured him. Not because she was afraid—she could take precautions as well as the next person—but because she already thought of it as something to share with Owen.

Dangerous thinking. Next thing she knew, she'd be weaving dreams that could have no possibility of ever coming true. Better to simply enjoy the moment and not think of what did, or did not, lie ahead.

"Let me help you with that," she said as he took the blanket from her and began spreading it out. The hike down to the beach had made them both hungry, and they made short work of opening the picnic basket. Owen had outdone himself with quantities of crisply fried chicken, biscuits that were still warm, fragrant slices of ham, even a honeyed mustard that bit the tongue before melting enticingly.

"I had a very small breakfast," Gwen explained as she succumbed to temptation and helped herself generously.

"I like a woman with a healthy appetite," he assured her. "After all, when a man's slaved over a hot stove, he wants to know his efforts are appreciated."

"Oh, I'd imagine yours always are," she said before realizing how that could be taken. When she did, she blushed, which made Owen throw back his head and laugh.

"How old are you that you can turn red like a schoolgirl?"

"Twenty-nine, and I'll have you know that blushing is a highly underrated art. How old are you?"

"Thirty-five, which I once thought was a great age, but I've since had to revise my opinions."

"I know what you mean," she said as she slipped a piece of ham between the two halves of a biscuit. "The closer I get to thirty, the younger it looks."

He laughed appreciatively. She looked very lovely with the sun gleaming off her coppery hair and the sparkle of pleasure in her gray-green eyes. The soft blue cotton shirt and jeans she wore revealed slender curves. She lay back on the blanket, propping herself up on an elbow, and he noted the gentle swell of her breasts where the shirt had been left open a few buttons.

"You're a beautiful woman," he said matter-of-factly as he continued to appraise her. "But you aren't overwhelmed by it. You seem comfortable with yourself."

"I don't know about the beautiful part," she said, "but you're right about the rest. I guess that's one of the benefits of getting older."

He nodded. "That and a few others, like getting to know what you really want."

"Have you done that?"

"To a certain extent. My life here suits me."

"Yet I hear you go off from time to time." She didn't know what prompted her to repeat what Daniel had said, simple curiosity, perhaps. She felt driven to know more about Owen.

He put down the chicken leg he had been about to bite into and looked at her carefully. "Who told you that? Wait, let me guess. It was Pierce."

"He mentioned it in passing," she admitted, then smiled. "He seems to regard you with suspicion, I suppose because you live differently from most people."

"Are you sure that's the only reason?"

"What do you mean?" she asked.

He hesitated, unsure of his ground and therefore of what he might say. "I don't know exactly. Only that he troubles me."

"Because he's so vehement about the direction Wales should take?"

"He's talked to you about that?"

"Some," she said. "I think he can't resist the subject. I admit his views on history appall me."

"He clearly doesn't subscribe to the view that those who ignore history are condemned to repeat it."

Gwen nodded. "I should have thought of saying that to him."

"I doubt he would have understood."

But Owen did. He was capable of cherishing the past even as he built for the future. In the final analysis that took far greater strength of character than Daniel's approach.

That thought made it a little easier for Gwen to accept how attracted she was to a man she had only just met and from whom she would shortly be parted.

"Care to do some exploring?" he asked when they had finished lunch. Gwen was still lying back on the blanket, looking up drowsily at the sky. She couldn't remember the last time she had felt so content.

Being with Owen was a constant series of contrasts: excitement and relaxation; security and anticipation. She had the feeling that even if she spent decades with him, she would never grow tired of his presence.

Barely had that idea surfaced than she was scrambling to her feet, eager for any distraction. "Sure, where did you have in mind?"

"This way," he said, rising more slowly, so that his long, hard body appeared to unfold gracefully. With one hand he indicated the farther reaches of the beach. "But bring your shoes. We'll be doing some climbing."

"Nothing too arduous, I hope. Not on a full stomach."

He took her hand with a reassuring grin. "I think you're up to it."

His estimation of her abilities was somewhat greater than Gwen's own, yet she managed to scramble after him up the side of the cliff toward what appeared at first to be merely a shadow on its face, but turned out, instead, to be a break in the limestone.

"This coastline is riddled with caves," he explained as he bent low to enter the narrow recess. The flashlight he had taken from the picnic basket shone a thin beam of light ahead of them.

Gwen followed more reluctantly. She had never been in a cave before and associated such places with bats and other creepy things she had no particular desire to meet. But there was no sign, at least at first glance, of any such inhabitants.

"Are we looking for the dragon?" she asked. "He'd have to be awfully small to live in here."

In fact, she had to stay partly stooped in order to avoid striking her head against the ceiling, from which pointed stalactites dripped. Owen, who was almost a foot taller, almost had to bend double.

"Winny told me," he said, "that there's supposed to be a passage through to a larger cave where the dragon lives. Trouble is, no one seems to know how to find it."

"That's okay by me," Gwen assured him. "I'd just as soon not impose on any dragons. But," she added after a moment, "if the only way in and out is a hidden passage, how does the dragon come and go?"

"By magic, of course," Owen said. He shone the flashlight along the far wall, where toadstools and other grayish-white fungi grew in abundance. "Fresh water must get in here somehow. Otherwise they couldn't live."

"How nice for them," Gwen murmured. She was beginning to feel a distinct chill, a sharp contrast to the

warmth and sunshine from which they had come.
Owen might think caves were great places to explore,
but they didn't rate high on her list.

She was about to say so when she realized that his
attention had been distracted by something near the
base of the wall. He was staring intently and moving
the flashlight back and forth in a shallow arc.

"What is it?" she asked.

"Nothing . . . I think."

He sounded so doubtful that she stepped closer for
a better look, but all she could make out on the sandy
floor were a series of scuff marks and twin tracks
about eighteen inches apart and an inch or so wide.
Nothing to excite her interest.

Owen bent over and picked something up which he
slid into his pocket. For a moment his face was blank;
then he appeared to register her puzzlement and discomfort.

"I'm sorry," he said. "You're not enjoying this.
Let's go back outside."

"It's all right."

He didn't seem to hear her, and took her arm and
escorted her from the cave. Gwen couldn't deny that
she was relieved to be back once more in the open air.
Something about the dank limestone interior had
given her the willies.

"Do many people go spelunking around here?" she
asked as they started back down the beach. As soon as
they reached the beach she took her shoes off again,
enjoying the feel of the sand between her toes.

"What's that?" Owen asked. "No, they don't. There are far more spectacular caves in other parts of Wales and Britain, so I suppose anyone who's interested goes there."

Though he'd answered her readily enough, he still seemed preoccupied. Gwen vaguely resented that, even though it amused her to realize how much she wanted his attention.

"Come on," she said, running ahead. "I'll race you back."

Taking him by surprise, she got the lead, but was hard-pressed to keep it. A glance over her shoulder showed Owen quickly gaining, though he didn't completely close the gap between them until she had almost reached the blanket. Then he lunged suddenly, a steely arm closing around her waist as together they fell laughing onto the sand.

Gwen lay on her back, looking up at him. There was something undeniably erotic about being chased down by a man, even in fun. It wasn't the sort of thing she would have expected to enjoy, but, then, she was discovering all sorts of feelings she hadn't known she possessed.

His eyes, thickly fringed by dark lashes, were the same crystalline azure as the sky. She watched, mesmerized, as his nostrils flared slightly. His firm lips were parted just enough for her to glimpse the whiteness of his teeth. A pulse beat in his square jaw, already lightly shaded by a few hours growth of beard.

"Gwen," he murmured thickly, "how you tempt me."

She could have assured him that it was mutual, except that she couldn't find the breath to speak. His weight gently pushing her down into the sand, his warmth invading every pore of her skin, his sheer masculinity making her vividly aware of her own vulnerability, all enthralled her.

When he bent his head and his mouth touched hers, his tongue instantly demanding entrance, she yielded without a second thought.

Lost in a world of their own creation, neither was aware of the man watching them from the cliff, his hands clenched at his sides and his face set.

Chapter 6

Owen raised his head and stared down at her, his eyes narrowed by desire, his chest rising and falling sharply against her soft breasts.

He was frightened. Not physically, which he would have been able to cope with, but emotionally, on a deeply rooted psychological level that defied control.

He had almost managed to convince himself that what he had felt when he first met her had been illusion, a fanciful overreaction brought on by the long-term lack of a woman in his life.

Celibacy didn't suit him any more than it would any other vigorous male uninspired by holy vows. But the alternatives, at least so far as he had experienced them, were equally unappealing.

He had long since passed through the phase of being satisfied merely to bed a woman, and had progressed to a need for a genuine, lasting relationship. That none had yet materialized left a gap in his life whose existence he could not ignore, yet neither could he pretend that Gwen could fill it.

She would be going away soon, back to her life in America. She had made that quite clear—which made her all the more dangerous to his mind and his heart. Too bad certain other parts of his body didn't understand that.

"Owen..."

The whisper of his name on her lips sent a tremor through him. He bent to capture the sweet sound, tasting the moist velvet of her mouth with deep, powerful strokes evocative of an even more intimate possession.

Gwen's slender arms clung to his broad back, her nails digging into the taut skin beneath his shirt. Scant layers of fabrics separated them, but they might have been suits of armor for all the frustration they caused. Helplessly she moaned with the urgency of her need and twisted beneath him.

Owen stifled a curse. What she did to his body stunned him. He was painfully hard with need, his blood thick and hot. The restraints of civilization, even of simple decorum, were rapidly breaking down. In another moment he would be pushing aside their clothes and taking her right there on the windswept beach.

He didn't want that. When they made love—he had to think of it as *when*, rather than *if*—it should be perfect. A large, cool bed in a shadowed room, and all the time in the world to discover each other. He wanted to hear her moans of pleasure, to witness her abandonment, to surrender himself in turn to the joy he did not doubt they would find together.

Abruptly he pulled himself off her and stood up. She blinked, dazed, as she stared at him, his silhouette dark against the sun. The warmth of his body still clung to hers, but she was suddenly bereft and, lying at his feet, almost terrifyingly vulnerable.

Then he held out a hand, and she automatically took it, rising to stand beside him. "Let's go," he said as he reached for the picnic basket. She nodded and bent to retrieve the blanket.

Hand in hand they climbed back up the path to where they had left the Jeep. Owen didn't speak again until they were on the road; then he said, "We're going to my place. We have to talk." A pulse leaped in his tightly clenched jaw.

Under any other circumstances Gwen would have strongly resented such high-handedness, but now she found herself mutely acceding. Was that what truly wanting a man did to a woman? Did it make her a pliant creature, easily led?

The idea wryly amused her, since it was so alien to her nature. She had the feeling that with Owen she would prove to be anything but pliant. He brought out her most aggressive impulses and filled her mind with visions that made her cheeks burn.

They eyed each other warily across the kitchen table. Lancelot had greeted them sleepily but not stirred from the yard. The chickens scratched the dirt around their coop. Off in the distance, a cow lowed.

Owen ran a hand through ebony hair already disheveled by the wind. Gwen made no effort to speak, causing him to realize how potent silence could be in a woman.

Yet he didn't fool himself into thinking that she was comfortable with the situation. He could only hope that they were both bothered by the same problem, and therefore might have a chance of finding a solution..

"Gwen," he said slowly, picking his words with great care, "I'm not a kid anymore. What was good enough for me once isn't worth having now."

He paused, waiting for her to speak. When she didn't, except with her large, eloquent eyes, which were watching him warily, he took a deep breath and went on. "I've passed the point of casual relationships."

"So have I," she said softly, the words little more than a whisper on the still air between them. A faint, rueful smile curved her mouth, swollen from his impassioned kisses. "Actually, they were never for me."

He nodded, relieved to hear that, even though it confirmed what he had suspected about her from the beginning. She had too much respect for herself to ever share her body lightly.

"I think," he said, "that we could have something very special."

Her eyes met his across the expanse of well-worn oak. "Yes."

His chest was so tight that it hurt. He had to clasp his hands together under the table to resist the urge to reach for her. Yet despite his raging hunger for her, some remnant of his sense of humor remained intact.

He glanced around the kitchen wryly. "This is hardly the place for a romantic tête-à-tête."

"I've noticed," Gwen said, "that when it comes to the really important things in life, the setting doesn't matter." Which was as close as she would come to admitting that, when she was with him, she was oblivious to their surroundings.

It was his turn to wait, sensing that she was on the verge of saying more.

"I've been thinking about Myrddin's Rock," she finally said. "Trying to figure out if it might somehow make sense to keep it. Unfortunately," she went on before he could comment, "I don't see how it would. Besides the question of being able to afford it, I couldn't be here more than a few weeks each year."

"Unless you moved to Wales."

"And did what? Assistant curators of medieval art are hardly in great demand."

Owen had a very clear idea of what she might do, but he knew that it was too early to mention it. Life had long ago accustomed him to being able to leap ahead, to see possibilities and take chances where others feared to tread.

Gwen was more cautious, one of the reasons he suspected they would get along so well. Their personalities complemented each other. She reminded him in certain ways of a particularly beautiful female hawk he had found the year before and nursed back to health. It had taken him months to win Artemis's trust. With Gwen, he had far less time.

"I understand what you're saying," he told her, "but I'd still like you to reconsider selling. There are ... things you don't know about yet."

"What do you mean?"

"Let me try to explain about the house," he said. "And please, bear with me, because I know what I'm going to say isn't going to make much sense to you."

Her curiosity caught despite herself, Gwen nodded. She leaned back in her chair and waited, but otherwise gave him no encouragement.

In fact, Owen needed little. He had gone over the tale so many times in his own mind that he could relate it in his sleep. His only problem was how to tell it in such a way that it would be believed. The best approach seemed to be the most straightforward.

"A few months ago," he began, "when Winny realized that she had only a little time left, she asked me to come see her. We had become good friends over the years, and I was in the habit of dropping in on her regularly just to make sure everything was all right, but she made a special point of that meeting.''

"I'm glad she had you," Gwen said softly.

"I enjoyed being with her," Owen said, making it clear that he didn't consider his concern for an elderly lady an act of charity. "She was intelligent and courageous right to the end, and she knew so much about this land. It was always fascinating to listen to her.

"At any rate," he continued, "what she had to tell me that evening was more than I'd bargained for. If I hadn't known Winny as well as I did, I'd have thought she was either the victim of a hoax or simply losing her wits."

"Go on," Gwen urged, her interest caught.

"She began by telling me about you and explaining a little of your background. It worried her that the two parts of your family had been out of touch for so long. She was afraid you would have no interest in Wales, or in the house."

He paused, as though inviting her to deny it. Honesty forced Gwen to speak the truth. "It's not that I have no interest, only that my life is elsewhere. Or at least," she added so softly that he almost missed it, "it has been."

"What does that mean?"

"I don't know. I'm trying to be sensible about this whole situation, but it's hard."

"Yes," he agreed gently, "I know it is."

They looked at each other for a long moment before Owen managed to drag his errant thoughts back to the matter at hand. "At any rate, Winny had considered writing down what she had to say in a letter to you, but no matter how she tried, she couldn't find a way to make it sound believable. So she decided to simply pass it along to me and let me pick the right moment to tell you."

"When is that going to be?" Gwen asked with a slight smile. She enjoyed a mystery as much as the next person, but she didn't particularly want to spend all afternoon talking about the house, not when they had more personal matters to discuss.

Owen looked taken aback for a moment, then laughed. Winny had often teased him, but not very many other women ever had. He found that he liked the experience.

"I'm getting there," he assured her. "You know that Myrddin's Rock is very old?"

Gwen nodded. "The tower appears to be pre-Norman."

"Definitely, but it was built on the site of an earlier house, a wooden hall—or more accurately, a series of halls—that housed generations of the Llywelyn chieftains. As unlikely as it may sound, Winny was convinced that your direct ancestors had ruled this land going back well into the first millenium, following the fall of the Roman Empire."

Gwen's eyebrows rose. "That's a real long shot. Few families have managed to hold onto land for more than four or five generations."

"You're right, but this was definitely an exception, and Winny claimed to know why." He took a deep breath, then said, "Family legend had it that Myrddin's Rock and the Llywelyns themselves are protected by a powerful magic spell cast by Myrddin—that is, by Merlin—shortly before his own disappearance. I don't say his death, because supposedly he lives on, in a sort of suspended animation, waiting for the right circumstances to revive him."

"What an, uh, interesting story."

"I'm not suggesting that you should take it at face value," he hastened to explain. "At any rate, the part about Merlin isn't really what's important. It's the reason for him casting the spell in the first place that matters. Supposedly he hid something of great value in the caves beneath the house. The Llywelyns are its guardians, with a little help from the dragon, of course."

"Winny actually believed this?" Gwen couldn't reconcile that with what she had come to imagine had been the character of her late relative. Surely she hadn't lost her faculties before she died?

"I think most of her life Winny tended to simply ignore the legend," Owen said. "But as she grew older, she came to perceive certain things that had previously been invisible to her."

"I don't understand what you mean," Gwen said, which was putting it mildly.

"Haven't you ever noticed that about old people?" Owen asked. "The best of them accept the inevitability of death with a gracefulness and courage that are rather breathtaking. They slip out of this life—and into the next—as naturally as you or I would walk from one room to the other. At some point they begin to almost straddle the two planes of existence, and when that happens they can understand things we can't."

"I guess...I've never talked to anyone about dying."

Owen smiled faintly. "It's the last taboo, isn't it?"

"You have to admit, it's hardly pleasant."

"Yet it happens to all of us," he pointed out. "Birth and death are the two experiences everyone on this planet shares. No matter what our differences, we're all bound together by how we come into this world and how we leave. That's the source of our common humanity."

"Most people," ventured Gwen, "prefer to simply ignore the subject."

"That's up to them, but it's certainly shortsighted. At any rate, Winny was concerned about what would happen afterward. Not to her, but to you."

Gwen frowned. "Why me? Even if she did take the legend about Merlin seriously, how could that pose any threat to me?"

Owen hesitated. He was treading on very thin ice. What he had to tell her was so unlikely—so preposterous, even—that he wouldn't blame her for scoffing at both it and him. Yet he had promised Winny that he would, at the least, communicate her concern.

"The legend," he said slowly, "says that the Llywelyns are the trustees of Merlin's treasure, whatever that may be. And if they fail at that responsibility, they will be destroyed."

"Are you seriously suggesting that I could be in danger?"

"No," Owen assured her quickly. "I don't completely discount what Winny told me, but I can't go so far as to believe all of it, either. Logically, what the legend probably means is that there is—or at one time was—something of value hidden in the caves under the house, and that the earliest of the Llywelyns were sworn to protect it. Anything beyond that, I have trouble swallowing."

Gwen was glad to hear it. At least that proved they weren't on completely different wavelengths. "It was kind of you to listen to Winny," she said, "and to agree to give me her message, but . . ."

He put his elbows on the table and leaned toward her urgently. "Gwen, just because neither you nor I can believe what Winny said, that doesn't mean we should ignore it. What she was really trying to get across to you is that you're the last of the Llywelyns and, as such, you should think long and hard before selling off your family legacy."

"She didn't have to concoct a silly fantasy to try to get me to stay."

"She didn't concoct it," Owen insisted. "After a lifetime of living in that house, she came to the conclusion that there was something to it. Enough at least that she felt she had to warn you."

Gwen stared over his shoulder into the middle distance, struggling to get her thoughts in order. She was distracted by what he had just told her, and mildly perturbed, but not enough to make her forget what had happened between them on the beach.

"Owen," she said finally, "if I were to consider keeping Myrddin's Rock—and I stress the *if*—it wouldn't be for any reason having to do with the past. As much as I respect what my ancestors did, I can't live my life on their terms."

"Good," he said, standing up and coming around to her side of the table. "Because I want you to consider keeping it for a very different reason."

She didn't have to ask what that was, not when his hands closed on her shoulders, gently drawing her up to him. Their bodies touched all along their lengths.

She felt the tensile strength of him, the male demand, and some deeply primitive force in her responded to it. Yet when his lips brushed hers it was not with the fierce passion they had shared earlier, but with a tender sweetness that in its own way was no less powerful.

"You know," she said when they at last drew shakily apart, "I can't make a decision about this now."

He nodded. "But we have at least a little time, don't we?"

Chapter 7

There you are, dear," Mrs. Gascoigne said as she placed the last of Gwen's purchases in the straw basket that had been the first of them. Paper bags were not in vogue in Castell Myrddin; shopping was done virtually daily and by the basketful, which afforded ample opportunity for the socializing Gwen was already beginning to enjoy.

Owen had offered to go with her, but she had declined, needing some time by herself. Every moment spent in his presence eroded her resolve not to do anything precipitous. Knowing that he was trying to avoid the same helped only a very little.

"Thank you," she said to the elderly shopkeeper. "I appreciate your help."

"Not at all, dear. I'm happy to do whatever I can for Winny's grandniece."

Gwen had picked up her basket and was about to turn away, when she paused and looked back at the tiny woman. Mrs. Gascoigne had spoken with such sincerity that Gwen was unable to doubt her. Her black eyes shone with understanding and something more, a willingness to help that Gwen could not ignore.

"Mrs. Gascoigne," she said slowly, "I take it you knew my great-aunt for a long time?"

"Oh, my, yes. We grew up together." She smiled reminiscingly. "Why, I remember the fun we had when we were both girls. To tell you the truth, we were both hell raisers. Why, there was the time the Gypsies camped near here and we went out to meet them. Two girls on their own weren't supposed to do that sort of thing, but we couldn't resist. There was an old woman who read our palms and told us what our futures held."

She chuckled softly to herself. "I call her an old woman, and she did seem ancient to us, but I'm older now than she was. I have a hard time believing that, since I still feel so young inside."

Gwen could well believe her. The spirit that looked out through those dark eyes was as youthful as Gwen's own. Had Winny's been the same?

When she asked Mrs. Gascoigne that, the old woman nodded vehemently. "Winny was never one to be weighed down by her years. She was active to the very end."

"Then she didn't . . . that is, her mind . . . ?"

"What about it?" the elderly lady asked challengingly.

"It was all right, at the end?"

Mrs. Gascoigne snorted. "Dear, there are young people I've known who would be doing very well to be as much in possession of their faculties as Winny was to the very last day of her life. She had a bright, inquiring mind that was always questioning, always wondering." A smile touched the withered features. "I like to think she's found some answers now."

"Better ones than the old Gypsy gave?" Gwen asked lightly. She was greatly relieved by what Mrs. Gascoigne had told her, not least because it corroborated what Owen had said.

"Actually," the shopkeeper said, "her predictions were remarkably accurate. Winny and I marveled over that more than once as our lives unfolded."

"I suppose she wasn't very specific."

"As a matter of fact, she was. She told me that I would marry young, have five children and lose one of them tragically. My eldest boy, William, died in the war. He was a navigator on a bomber that was shot down over Germany."

"I'm sorry," Gwen murmured.

Mrs. Gascoigne nodded, accepting her sympathy. "I can still see William as clearly as though he left here yesterday. He was always different from the other children, more alive, somehow, and eager to discover the world. My greatest consolation has been that he lived every moment of his life fully, short though it was.

"But enough of that," she went on, straightening her shoulders. "What the Gypsy said turned out to be true enough. She predicted that Winny would never marry, something I couldn't believe, since she was so lovely and any number of young men were interested in her. But back then marriage wasn't as good a deal for a woman as it is now. Winny preferred to keep her independence."

"Did she ever think about leaving here?" Gwen asked, resting her basket on the counter.

"Oh, but she did leave," Mrs. Gascoigne explained. "She went to school for several years in England and later traveled on the continent. Winny was no stick-in-the-mud, let me tell you, and the family was well off enough that she could have settled elsewhere if she had wished."

"But she never considered that?"

"Actually, I think she did, at least until Davey died."

"Davey? Who was he?"

Mrs. Gascoigne's eyes narrowed thoughtfully. "You've never heard him spoken of?"

Gwen shook her head. "Not that I can remember."

"He was your great-uncle, brother to both Winny and your grandfather. As the eldest son, he inherited Myrddin's Rock."

"Of course," Gwen murmured. "I should have realized that there must have been another son. That was why my grandfather left."

Mrs. Gascoigne nodded. "He was the youngest of the three. Winny was actually the eldest, but by tradition the property went to the first-born male. Davey, however, had no interest in the place."

"He didn't want to live there?"

"Couldn't bear the idea. It was the bright lights of London for him."

"What happened?"

"He came back briefly to straighten out his affairs here and was killed in an accident."

Gwen's throat tightened. She had to swallow hard before she asked, "What kind of accident?"

"No one ever knew exactly what happened. His body was found on the beach below the house. Speculation was that he'd fallen from the cliff."

"I see."

"It was very tragic, of course, though to be honest, people hereabouts hadn't thought all that much of Davey, and we weren't too surprised when he came to a bad end. For a while we thought your grandfather might return, but he was already building a life for himself in America and wanted to stay. That was fine, since Winny was willing to move back here."

So her great-aunt had returned to Myrddin's Rock and devoted the remainder of her long life to the house. Apparently she had been happy enough to do so, but Gwen couldn't help but wonder how much her decision had been colored by the circumstances of her brother's death. Was that when she had begun to believe that there was some strange force at work among the Llywelyns?

"Mrs. Gascoigne...did Winny ever talk to you about the early history of Myrddin's Rock, even going back before this house was built?"

"You mean back to the beginning?"

"Yes, did she speak of that?"

The old woman sighed. She eased her frail body onto a wooden stool and rubbed the bridge of her nose pensively. "Once, a few years ago. We went into Cardiff together to see that movie, *Camelot*. Winny found it quite amusing. It seemed she had done a lot of research about King Arthur and was convinced that the stories about him held a grain of truth, but that over the centuries the truth was mixed with details that didn't fit."

"Did she give you any examples?"

"Oh, yes. To begin with, he wasn't a medieval king. That's how he's presented, isn't it, dear? The castles and the knights, all that business in Malory, that's pure medievalism. Very romantic, but not accurate."

Gwen nodded slowly. "It's true that historians who are willing to grant that there may really have been a King Arthur think that he lived much earlier, back in the so-called Dark Ages."

"That's what Winny said. That he was really a clan chieftain who had tried to keep Britain united after the

Romans left. Perhaps he even succeeded for a while, but once he died, everything flew apart.''

"And only the legend was left," Gwen murmured. "Of a golden time when a great king kept the peace."

"Considering how hard life was back then—the lack of education, the terrible poverty and disease—you can't really blame people for exaggerating the truth and creating a myth around it."

"No," Gwen agreed, "of course not. But even if there was an Arthur, that doesn't mean there was ever a Merlin, or a Guinevere, or any of the others.

"I'm not so sure of that, dear. The human imagination is a wonderful thing, but I don't really believe the whole story of Camelot could have been invented, with only Arthur being the least bit true. Guinevere has always struck me as very real. There are women like her today, unable to be satisfied with what they have, no matter how good it is, and drawn to whatever happens to be forbidden. As for Merlin, he existed all right, although precisely what he was no one can now say for sure. Perhaps he was a priest of the old faith, from before Christianity, who had powers other people considered magical."

"Perhaps," Gwen agreed. If so, he had been caught in the powerful currents of history as the old ways yielded to the new. Surely many men like him must have resisted fiercely, whereas, if the legends were to be believed at all, Merlin had seen the future and tried to make it as good as possible.

"It occurred to me," she said slowly, "that it might not be coincidence that there was a monastery built near Myrddin's Rock. The early Christians had a habit of taking over older holy sites and claiming them as their own."

"I've heard that, too," Mrs. Gascoigne said. "But if it's true in this case, it raises an interesting point. Why didn't they take over Myrddin's Rock itself, instead of merely building nearby?"

"Because the Llywelyns were there?"

"Many Welsh families were dispossessed, no matter how strong they were or how hard they fought. Yet the Llywelyns remained."

Gwen had no explanation for her family's remarkable tenacity. What Mrs. Gascoigne said was certainly true: given every evidence of history, they should have been forced out long ago. Yet they had held on, down to the present time.

And when one of them had tried to reject his heritage, he had died.

Back on the street a short time later, Gwen shivered, despite the warm sunshine. She felt chilled to the very marrow of her bones, and telling herself that she was being foolish didn't help at all.

The news of her great-uncle's fate had come as a shock, but there was no reason to exaggerate its significance. For all she knew, Davey Llywelyn might have been a bit too fond of the bottle and tumbled from the cliff while intoxicated. Certainly that fit in with the image of a young man who preferred the social whirl of London to more mundane responsibilities at home.

Or were those responsibilities mundane? Had Davey been provoked by an awareness of something ancient and frightening with which he simply couldn't cope?

Her imagination was running riot. This was the twentieth century, not the tenth. She was a well educated, sensible woman who had seen men walk on the moon and took it for granted that human life could begin in a petri dish. It was absurd to think that she could be affected by the lingering magic of a figure wreathed in the mists of legend.

Yet what was magic, after all? If Merlin had existed, and if he were suddenly transported to her own time, wouldn't he be awed by the forces modern man controlled? What would he make of television, electric lights, vaccinations, nuclear weapons? His explanation for them might be quite different from the scientific "truth," yet in the final analysis it might be no less accurate. It wasn't beyond the scope of belief to think that there might be other forces that had once been recognized, but had become lost in the distant past, forces a man known as a magician might have been able to control.

Gwen looked absently up and down the street. The solid two-and three-story red brick buildings seemed to blur slightly, as though they weren't quite as solid as they had appeared. She blinked in an effort to clear her vision, but when she opened her eyes again it hadn't improved. She had a vague sense of sharp edges dissolving, molecules shifting, reality peeling away to reveal . . . what?

"Gwen," a voice said nearby, "are you all right?"

She took a deep breath and shook herself slightly. "Daniel . . . yes, I'm fine. I was just a little dizzy, that's all."

He frowned, taking her arm and leading her toward the pub next door, where several tables and chairs had been placed out in front. "You're white as a sheet, and trembling. Here, sit down."

She did as he said, aware that her legs were shaking. The firmness of the chair under her was reassuring, as was the table that she instinctively grasped. "I don't know what came over me."

"Do you feel ill? I can get you to a doctor."

She shook her head, touched by his concern. He was leaning forward anxiously, his eyes glued to her face, which she supposed was as pale as he had said. Certainly she still felt chilled, though not as much as she had a few moments before.

"Thank you," she said, "but that isn't necessary. I'm probably just tired from my trip." She smiled wanly. "I'm not a terribly good traveler."

"Still, you should be over that by now. Have you been eating properly?"

"As a matter of fact, I did skip breakfast this morning."

"Then you must have something. Wait here a moment." He disappeared into the pub, returning almost at once with a tray holding two mugs of beer and a plate of sandwiches. "Not the best food in the world," he said as he set the plate and one of the mugs in front of her, "but it will fill you up."

"That's very kind of you, Daniel, but . . ."

"No buts. Eat. You looked as though you were about to faint back there."

"I never faint," she told him as she picked up one of the sandwiches. It was filled with some unidentifiable meat, and the bread was soggy, but she was hungry enough not to mind.

"Living in that barn of a place must be getting you down," he said. "It can't be what you're used to."

"That's true," Gwen agreed between bites. "But it has a certain charm." Which, she realized with a start, was true. Even with the erratic plumbing, the earth tremors and the nest of spiders she had discovered that morning in the closet, she was becoming quite fond of Myrddin's Rock.

"I'll be sure to stress that in the advertisements," Daniel told her with a grin.

"About those . . ." She hesitated, unsure of what to say. Vague stirrings and chaotic thoughts had not yet formed themselves into anything remotely resembling an actual decision, and might not, since it could only weigh against her better judgment.

Nonetheless she said, "I've been thinking, Daniel. There might be some way I could hold on to the house, and I may decide that I'd like to do that, at least for a while."

"I don't understand," he said, reaching into his jacket pocket for a wrinkled pack of cigarettes. He lit one and looked at her through a cloud of smoke.

She smiled tentatively. "I'm not sure I do, either, only that the old place seems to be growing on me."

"The place, or—"

She knew what he was about to say and determinedly cut him off. "I like the house, Daniel, but even if I didn't the fact is that when I came here I didn't really understand what it meant. Winny's leaving it to me is something very important. I can't be in such a hurry to walk away."

It struck her as ironic that she should say those words first to Daniel, who didn't want to hear them, rather than to Owen, who did. But, then, it was easier to disappoint Daniel than give in to Owen. Because once she gave in, once she took the first step, she had no doubt where it would lead.

At least she no longer looked pale. Despite the cooling breeze, she could feel the flush warming her cheeks. She remembered how Owen had teased her about blushing, and that reddened her skin even further. How deliciously absurd for a woman her age to blush at the thought of a man. And how much better than the casual, even blasé attitudes she had seen her friends affect to hide their inner confusion and hurt.

"You're looking better," Daniel said grudgingly. He stubbed the cigarette out and took a long swallow of his beer, looking at her over the rim of the mug. "But

I can't believe that you really mean what you say. It's just a novelty to you. In time you'll—"

"Daniel," she said gently, "you're being patronizing. I assure you, I'm quite capable of making up my own mind. I may still decide to sell. And I realize that if I don't, you stand to lose a sizable commission."

"That's not what I'm concerned about," he insisted with injured dignity.

"I'm sorry...." She really did seem to have misjudged him.

"I'm only worried about your getting hurt."

For a moment she thought he was referring to the legend of the vengeful dragon, but instead he said, "Owen Garrett isn't to be trusted."

Gwen resisted the impulse to spring to Owen's defense. She was surprised by the vehemence of her own feelings and felt compelled to mask them. Mildly she said, "That's a rather serious charge to make."

"Nevertheless, it's what I believe." His chin jutted out stubbornly, as though prepared for a blow.

"On what grounds?" She didn't mean to sound as though she were cross-examining him, but she was curious to know the source of his dislike for Owen.

"He...there's too much about him that's unexplained."

Gwen resisted the urge to smile. Daniel was undeniably well educated in the legal profession, but he had lived most of his life in a very small town and had what she thought of as the insular prejudices of people who had experienced relatively little of the larger world.

She was no stranger to that phenomenon herself, having encountered it even in as seemingly sophisticated a place as Cambridge. If it could exist there, she took it for granted that it could exist in a small Welsh village.

"Everyone has secrets," she said gently.

He shot her a sharp look. "You seem very straightforward."

"I'm not sure that's a compliment."

"I meant it as one," he assured stiffly. "I don't want to see you get hurt."

He had reached out and covered her hand with his own. There was nothing overtly unpleasant about his touch; it wasn't too personal or presumptuous. Yet Gwen had to fight the desire to pull away. She was beginning to sense an intensity in him that seemed to stem from the same source as his political convictions, but that was more intimately directed at her, and that worried her.

"Daniel, I appreciate your concern, but I really don't believe Owen poses any threat to me." That wasn't quite true, since he certainly threatened her equilibrium, but she wasn't about to admit that.

"I hope you're right," he said slowly. "I want to believe that, but..."

"But what?" she asked.

He looked away, staring at something she couldn't see. "We live in such a violent world. It breeds violence. Sometimes a man can't help what he does."

Gwen was confused. Was he still talking about Owen, or about someone else? Himself? That didn't make any sense. What did a country lawyer know about violence? Whereas Owen . . . she could believe that he had some inner understanding of it.

There was something about him—a barely restrained sense of power, a keen edge of danger—that made her able to see him in situations where she could not imagine Daniel. She remembered the hard strength of his body and the graceful agility of his movements, remembered how it felt to be touched by him, and how much she wanted to touch in return.

A shadow passed over the sun, and she shivered.

Chapter 8

That afternoon, driven by a certain confusion of the spirit, Gwen got into her rented car and went for a solitary ramble. She had no particular destination in mind—except to leave the island for a while—nor did she need any. It was enough to tool along the largely deserted roads, enjoying the countryside, the crystal clear day and her own company, free of the complexities created by man.

From a distance she saw the looming mass of Castle Caernarvon, famed for its thirteen polygonal towers and its red sandstone ramparts. For over seven hundred years it had proclaimed the English presence in Wales, and it still looked, even to the modern eye, to be a formidable declaration of the intent to hold on to what had been so bloodily won. She thought of Daniel's rage and felt some small glimmer of understanding.

She stopped at a roadside pub for dinner and was pleased to discover that a woman dining alone was no more likely to be bothered there than in the more enlightened establishments of Boston. Indeed, she was granted a degree of courtesy and privacy she had learned not to take for granted anywhere.

It was fully dark by the time she returned to Angelsey and Myrddin's Rock, and she had to use her high beams to find the turnoff onto her road. Then she had to make her way to the front door in suffocating darkness and found it finally only by holding her hands out in front of her blindly.

Vowing that her next purchase would be a flashlight for the glove compartment, she fumbled the key into the lock and let herself in with a sigh of relief, which gave way almost instantly to a groan of dismay when she flipped the light switch without result.

"Oh, no..." Hard on complete exasperation came the realization that she should have expected something like this. After all, problems were cropping up one after another in the old house. Why should the wiring be exempt?

In Cambridge she had been through two blackouts following severe storms and found them rather amusing, excuses for neighbors to get together and entertain one another. In her small apartment she'd had no trouble finding candles and a flashlight, and she'd always had a battery-powered radio on hand.

This time she had nothing, at least, not that she could reach. Being a nonsmoker, she didn't even have a pack of matches, which left her with only one source of light—the car.

Muttering to herself, she stumbled back down the path, got behind the wheel and turned the engine on. With the help of the headlights and a fine disregard for the suspension, she maneuvered the car out of the driveway and around the back of the house. There she parked it with the engine still going, reasoning that she could get in through the back door to the kitchen, where she would be able to see well enough to at least find the candles she seemed to remember were in one of the drawers.

They were, but the match holder by the stove was empty; she had used the last one that morning.

"Damn," she murmured to herself.

Winny had kept extra supplies in a small storeroom off the kitchen. It was down a rickety flight of wooden steps. Unfortunately the headlights' beams did not extend that far. Taking a deep breath, she grasped hold of the stair railing and cautiously put her foot on the first step. By sliding first one foot forward and then the other, she got what she estimated was halfway down. In daylight the distance was nothing, but in complete darkness it was more than a little intimidating. She paused for a moment, feeling the rapid movement of her heart against her ribs, then went on.

She stepped into nothingness. Her foot pushed through empty air, her hand tore lose from the banister, and the rest of her body followed. She fell into blackness, landing on hard-packed earth. Stars whirled before her. There was a great rushing in her ears, and everything she knew of the world vanished.

Owen walked up the path slowly. By the light of the rising moon he could make out Myrddin's Rock straight ahead. No lights were showing, nor could he see Gwen's car, and he wondered where she might be at such a late hour.

He knew where he was supposed to be, at home in bed, preferably asleep. That he was not both baffled and annoyed him. He had spent a productive enough evening, catching up on various things that needed to be done. When he finally got off the phone with Cardiff, he had poured himself a brandy and put his feet up on his desk, a favorite position for thinking.

When he had done enough of that he went for a walk with Lancelot, checked the animals for the night and settled down in bed with the latest thriller by a bestselling novelist who had let it be understood that he had connections in the world of terrorism that allowed him to write with special authority. Owen enjoyed his work because of its gross inaccuracies.

He had drifted into sleep, only to awake suddenly with a distinct sense of unease. Long years of training, not to mention experience, had him reaching for the gun beside the bed even before he was fully awake.

He sat up, penetrating the darkness with all his senses until he was convinced that whatever had awakened him was not close at hand.

Slowly he got out of bed and stood naked in the faint light, a dull metallic glint betraying the presence of the gun in his hand. Still nothing, except the definite impression that any further attempts at sleep would be futile. At certain times in his life Owen had learned to simply listen to his instincts and not to waste any effort trying to understand them. That stood him in good stead now as he dressed quickly and left the house.

Without pausing to wonder why he was doing so, he headed toward Myrddin's Rock, only to stop finally as he approached it and found that Gwen was apparently not at home.

Was she with Daniel? The mere thought brought a light to his eyes that only a few people had ever seen, and none had lived to tell of. The sheer enormity of his own rage forced him to step back and examine his feelings. She was an independent woman with no ties to him; she had the right to do whatever she pleased. But if she was with the lawyer, Owen would waste no time taking her from him and making it very clear where she actually belonged.

His mouth set in a grim line, he advanced on the house, intending to wait there until she came home. And she could damn well make of that whatever she wanted to. To his surprise he found the kitchen door unlocked. Many people in the country didn't bother much with security, but he couldn't believe that Gwen, being from the big city, would be so careless. Owen slid his hand under the tweed jacket he wore and let his fingers curl around the gun.

It was dark inside but he made no attempt to turn on the lights. The dimness didn't trouble him; he moved through it easily and without a sound.

Through the window, he could see Gwen's car. The gun came out of its holster, along with a pencil thin flashlight. Its beam caught the open door to the storeroom. At the same time he heard a faint moan.

She was lying at the bottom of the stairs in a crumpled heap, with her face down and her hair spilling over the earthen floor. Owen felt a flash of fear unlike anything he had ever experienced for himself. He took the steps on the run, leaping over the one halfway down that had broken through and ignoring the torn railing, except to note it in passing.

Kneeling beside her, he forced himself not to attempt to turn or lift her immediately. Instead his hands moved over her swiftly, allowing him to ascertain the extent of her injuries as best he could.

When he was satisfied that neither her neck nor her back was broken, nor any limbs, he turned her gently. She felt very light in his arms. He rose and carried her back up the stairs, going on without pause until he reached the tower bedroom. There he lowered her to the bed and flipped the switch on the lamp beside the bed. Nothing happened.

SILHOUETTE

 PRESENTS

A
Real Sweetheart
of a Deal!

**7
FREE
GIFTS**

**PEEL BACK
THIS CARD
AND SEE
WHAT YOU
CAN GET!
THEN...**

Complete the Hand Inside

*It's easy! To play your cards right,
just match this card with the cards
inside.*

Turn over for more details . . .

Incredible isn't it? Deal yourself in <u>right now</u> and get 7 fabulous gifts.
ABSOLUTELY FREE.

1. 4 BRAND NEW SILHOUETTE INTIMATE MOMENTS NOVELS – FRE
Sit back and enjoy the excitement, romance and thrills of fo
fantastic novels. You'll receive them as part of this winning strea

2. A BEAUTIFUL AND PRACTICAL PEN AND WATCH – FREI
This watch with its leather strap and digital read-out certainly loo
elegant – but it is also extremely practical. Its quartz crystal mov
ment keeps precision time! And the pen with its slim good looks w
make writing a pleasure.

3. AN EXCITING MYSTERY BONUS – FREE!
And still your luck holds! You'll also receive a special mystery bon
You'll be thrilled with this surprise gift. It will be the source of mar
compliments as well as a useful and attractive addition to your hom

PLUS

**THERE'S MORE. THE DECK IS STACKED IN YOUR FAVOR. HER
ARE THREE MORE WINNING POINTS. YOU'LL ALSO RECEIVI**

4. A MONTHLY NEWSLETTER – FREE!
It's "Heart to Heart" – the insider's privileged look at our most popul
writers, upcoming books and even recipes from your favorite autho

5. CONVENIENT HOME DELIVERY
Imagine how you'll enjoy having the chance to preview the roman
tic adventures of our Silhouette heroines in the convenience o
your own home at less than retail prices! Here's how it works. Ever
month we'll deliver 4 new books right to your door. There's no obli
gation and if you decide to keep them, they'll be yours for onl
$2.49! That's 26¢ less per book than what you pay in stores. An
there's no extra charge for postage and handling.

6. MORE GIFTS FROM TIME TO TIME – FREE!
It's easy to see why you have the winning hand. In addition to all th
other special deals available only to our home subscribers, you ca
look forward to additional free gifts throughout the year.

SO DEAL YOURSELF IN – YOU CAN'T HELP BUT WIN

You'll Fall In Love
With This Sweetheart Deal
From Silhouette!

SILHOUETTE BOOKS
FREE OFFER CARD

**4 FREE BOOKS • DIGITAL WATCH AND MATCHING PEN
• FREE MYSTERY BONUS • INSIDER'S NEWSLETTER •
HOME DELIVERY • MORE SURPRISE GIFTS**

☐ *YES! Deal me in. Please send me four free Silhouette Intimate Moments novels, the pen and watch and my free mystery gift as explained on the opposite page.*   240 CIL YAA2

First Name	Last Name
PLEASE PRINT	

Address		Apt.

City	State

Zip Code

Offer limited to one per household and not valid for present subscribers. Prices subject to change.

SILHOUETTE NO RISK GUARANTEE

- There is no obligation to buy – the free books and gifts remain yours to keep.
- You pay the lowest price possible – and receive books before they're available in stores.
- You may end your subscription at any time – just let us know.

PRINTED IN U.S.A.

Remember! To win this hand, all you have to do is place your sticker inside and DETACH AND MAIL THE CARD BELOW. You'll get four free books, a free pen and watch and a mystery bonus.

BUT DON'T DELAY! MAIL US YOUR LUCKY CARD TODAY!

If card has been removed write to:

Silhouette, 901 Fuhrmann Blvd., P.O. Box 9013, Buffalo, N.Y. 14240-9013

With a low curse he raced back down the stairs and found the candles he knew Winny kept in the kitchen. Back in the bedroom, he set up several and lit them with the lighter he habitually carried for no other reason than that a source of fire was often useful.

In the candlelight he could make out the ashen pallor of Gwen's skin and the shallowness of her breathing. There was an ugly bruise on her forehead, but otherwise he could find no visible injuries.

His hands were shaking as he carefully undressed her, checking each part of her body as it was revealed to him. Her arms were discolored where she had used them to try to break her fall. Above the swell of her left breast was an abrasion that made him wince as he uncovered it.

Considering that he had seen vastly worse injuries, and even suffered them himself, his response to what had happened to her was uncharacteristically severe. It was all he could do not to gather her up in his arms again and hold her close, trying to keep her safe, however belatedly, from every danger.

Instead he found a nightgown in a drawer and slipped her into it, then covered her gently. Checking her pulse, he made the decision not to send for a doctor. The nearest one was some twenty miles away and not regarded as particularly reliable. His own medical training was extensive enough for him to be confident of his ability to care for her.

He sat down on the bed beside her, holding her hand and watching until he was satisfied that she had slipped into a natural sleep. Only then did he go back downstairs to do something else he had been trained for.

A quick search outside the house located the main power lines. Instead of running inside through the meter, they lay on the ground nearby. He didn't touch them, suspecting that they were still alive, but he looked closely enough to determine that they looked torn from their connectors rather than simply cut.

Clever. Cut wires would arouse suspicion and invite questions, whereas wires torn loose could be explained away by any number of natural phenomena, from poor weather and wild animals to fallen trees. And in fact there was an old oak lying nearby, its dead branches testifying to the ease with which it could have brought the wires down.

All very logical, except that Owen didn't happen to believe it. He saw the faint traces of footprints around the wires and suspected that a human agency had been involved. But why? For what purpose would anyone want to black out Myrddin's Rock? And how intentional had Gwen's fall been? It looked like a genuine accident, but accidents were chancy things. Would whoever had been behind this be back to check on the effectiveness of his handiwork?

Of course, there was always the possibility that he was wrong. Whatever arrogance he might once have possessed had long since been burned out of him. In its place was a confidence that allowed him to accept the possibility of error and assess it carefully.

The shoe prints might have been caused by anyone passing by, a repairman from the phone company, for instance, or simply a hiker who wasn't being overly scrupulous about private property. The tree might very well have brought the wires down, and it could have fallen for any number of reasons. Or perhaps a dragon had blown it over.

Shaking his head ruefully, he returned to the house and carefully examined the stairs leading to the storeroom. The wood was old and inclined to crumble easily, but there was no indication that they had been tampered with. He would have to speak with Gwen about replacing them with stone steps. The banister that had torn loose had been attached to the wall with iron screws, long since corroded. It wasn't difficult to imagine them working loose.

So perhaps it had been an accident, after all. He had no solid evidence to the contrary, but on the other hand, the faint prickling at the back of his neck warned him that something was wrong. Until he was convinced that no malignant agency, human or otherwise, was responsible for what had happened to Gwen, he intended to keep a very close watch over her.

Which meant that he wasn't going anywhere that night.

Back in the bedroom, he checked her carefully and was reassured that she continued to sleep. Her temperature, pulse and breathing were normal. He told himself that she would be fine, and that the smartest thing he could do was get some sleep himself.

Stretched out in a nearby chair, he watched her by the dim moonlight for some time before his eyelids finally grew heavy and he drifted away into uneasy dreams.

Gwen woke to a throbbing headache and the impression that a truck had run over her. She opened her eyes slowly, wincing as the bright sunlight struck them. Her lips were dry, and her tongue felt stuck to the top of her mouth. She was reluctant to move, anticipating that she would not appreciate the results. But a need to find out what had happened to her compelled her to raise her head.

That was a mistake. Barely had she lifted it from the pillow than the room swam before her eyes and bile rose in her throat. She moaned helplessly.

Instantly strong arms were around her. She was cradled against a rock-hard chest, and a low voice said soothingly, "It's all right. You'll be okay."

Confusion rippled through Gwen's mind, as uncomfortable in its own way as the pain that had preceded it. Who was this man? How had he gotten into her apartment? What did he have to do with whatever had happened to her?

"What...?" she began, barely recognizing the high, hesitant voice as her own. The man bent closer, and his face swam into view. With it came a blessed sense of recognition. "Owen."

"Shhh," he said gently. "Lie back down and I'll get you some water." It shook him to see how pale and weak she was, but he consoled himself that she would be better soon. At least she was fully conscious and aware of who he was. She had even seemed glad to see him.

She was looking at him bemusedly when he returned from the bathroom with a glass of water and a damp towel. She took a few sips, and, when she was done, he set the glass on the bedside table and gently wiped her face with the cool cloth.

She stiffened as he did so, surprised by his ministrations. "You don't have to..."

"It will make you feel better." He insisted on finishing, not satisfied until he saw a slight flush of color replace the pallor in her cheeks. She was looking at him with wide gray-green eyes in which apprehension lingered. The nightgown he had put her in had slipped off her shoulders. He could see the high, rounded curve of her breasts and the faint tracing of blue veins beneath her pale skin.

"Some tea would help, too," he said gruffly. "I'll fix it."

He turned to go. She held out a hand, touching his, stopping him. "Wait...Owen, what happened?"

"You fell down the storeroom steps. Banged your head. I came over and found you. You'll be all right."

She took a breath, her lips parted. She was about to speak, when he gently disengaged his hand and headed for the door. "I'll be back in a few minutes. Don't try to get out of bed by yourself."

Of course, she did. It was a mistake. She had barely gotten her legs over the side of the bed, when the dizziness hit her. Still, she persevered, forcing herself to stand, and even to take several steps before her legs gave way.

She was sitting on the stone floor, her nightgown spread around her like a white lacy cloud, a bewildered look on her face, when Owen returned.

He muttered something she was just as glad she couldn't understand and put the tea down on the bedside table with a loud thump. "For God's sake..." he said as he strode over and bent to lift her as easily as though she were a child. "Couldn't you stay put?"

She didn't bother to answer, too secure and comfortable in his arms to bestir herself to speak. Her eyes were closing again. She really was very tired.

Owen watched her sleep. He sat in the chair near the bed as the hours passed, his long legs stretched out in front of him and his head tilted back. Through half-shuttered eyes he studied the slow rise and fall of her breathing.

He was oddly content. It was enough to simply be watching over her. He was where he belonged. Later there would be things to do and say, but this small amount out of time he was satisfied to wait.

She was very lovely in a way that not only aroused his desire, but also provoked him to tenderness. He thought he could be perfectly content simply to walk and talk with her, learning to share her life with his own.

Then he smiled at his own romanticism. Certainly he wanted to do all those things. But he also wanted to make love to her.

In the afternoon Gwen awoke again. She was shy with him, but accepted his help in reaching the bathroom, though she insisted she was perfectly capable of taking a shower by herself. It had not escaped her notice that he had removed her clothes, and she was self-conscious enough about that.

He stayed in the bedroom while she showered, not leaving until she emerged wrapped in a blue silk robe with her damp hair curling around her shoulders. "All right?" he asked, trying not to stare too hard at the slender shape of her.

She nodded without meeting his eyes. "Fine."

"I'll go and fix you something to eat, then."

"You don't have to."

"I'll bring it up here. Don't try to come down."

She gave up trying to argue, mainly because she didn't want to. It was very... reassuring to be taken care of by him. It even felt quite natural.

She was sitting on the edge of the bed when he returned. She had dried her hair and put on a fresh nightgown, with the robe over it.

Owen stood in the door, looking at her. His hands clenched on the tray. She looked up, and their eyes met. He cleared his throat with some difficulty.

"Are you hungry?" he asked.

Her gaze did not waver from his. "Very."

Chapter 9

The blue-gray shadows of approaching dawn invaded the room gently, falling over the bed on which the man and woman lay. Gwen's head was pillowed on Owen's chest, her fingers tangled in the mat of ebony curls. Beneath the thin sheet his long leg was thrown over hers. Strands of her cinnamon-hued hair were caught in his large hands.

They slept deeply, exhausted by the passion that had drained them. Neither had expected it to be like that. Their hunger for each other had been all but insatiable. Again and again they had reached out, forgetting everything except the driving need to possess and be possessed.

Gwen stirred in her sleep. Her eyes flickered open and focused on the shadowed cleft of Owen's chin, darkened by the night's growth of whiskers. Her pupils dilated slightly as memories of the previous hours filtered back.

It had begun so tenderly. Owen had put down the tray—it was still on the dresser, forgotten—and come to sit beside her on the bed. His hand, when he reached out to brush her hair away from her bruised forehead, was infinitely gentle. He even smiled slightly.

She was watching his mouth, fascinated by the way it turned up at the corners and caused little lines to appear, when he said, "You make me nervous."

"What?"

"Nervous. I can't remember the last time a woman did that."

"Why should you be nervous?" she asked, startled into meeting his eyes. They were a darker blue than she had seen before, as though a storm were building behind them.

"Because," he murmured, tracing the line of her cheek down to her jaw, "I want this to be perfect."

"It already is," she said. He had the most incredible lashes, dark and thick, lashes a woman would have killed for. She wanted to touch them ever so lightly, to brush her lips over his eyelids, to learn with her hands and her mouth the contours of his face and his body. To truly know him with all her senses was a task that could take a lifetime, and one to which she would gladly devote herself.

The fleeting thought came as a shock because intimacy, particularly on the all-absorbing level she was thinking about, had never been easy for her. She had always held a great deal of herself in reserve, whether through some failure of desire or trust. Hence her less than grandiose expectations about lovemaking.

Owen was watching her carefully. He saw the shyness in her, and the restraint, as though she were afraid of expecting too much.

"Am I wrong to think," he asked gently, "that you haven't done this sort of thing very often?"

If he was mistaken, and there was some truly bad experience in her past, he wanted to know about it so that he could allay her fears. On the other hand, if his instincts were right and she was simply relatively inexperienced, he was less concerned. Still nervous, but also confident of his ability to give her pleasure.

She stiffened and turned her head away, staring unseeingly at the opposite wall. "The problem is," she said softly, "that I've never really understood what all the fuss is about. Once my initial curiosity was satisfied, I didn't have much motivation to get involved." She didn't add that she had found the whole business oddly disappointing. Her responses were normal enough, according to what she had heard and read. She simply didn't see what made sex worth the effort.

"Then you weren't in love with the man," Owen said.

She shrugged. "I suppose I didn't think love had much to do with it." Yet she must have learned better

somewhere along the way, because she hadn't repeated her one mistake, to the chagrin of poor Jeffrey and several other gentlemen of her acquaintance.

"What are you smiling about?" Owen asked.

"I was just thinking about how frustrating I must
have seemed."

He laughed and slipped an arm around her waist,
drawing her closer. Gently his mouth nuzzled the
silken length of her throat. "Let's just call you challenging."

Her head fell back against his shoulder as he sought
the scented hollow between her collarbones. When his
tongue darted out to stroke her lightly, she was hard-
pressed to stifle a moan. Huskily she asked, "Is that
how you see me? As a challenge?"

"No," he murmured, his mouth hot and seeking
against her skin. "You're a human being, a woman,
and, I hope, a friend. I want to make love with you,
not have sex. And I think you want the same."

"There's a difference . . . ?" she asked weakly.

"Oh, yes." He raised his head and looked at her
directly. "Trust me."

She did, and in the end nothing could have been
more natural. When he undid the tie of her robe and
gently slid it from her shoulders, she offered no ob-
jection. Through the thin fabric of her nightgown he
could see the fullness of her breasts, with their darkening nipples, the indentation of her waist and the
graceful curve of her hips. Gently, but with unmis-

takable directness, he placed his hand over her belly above the shadowed triangle that hid her femininity.

His touch there, warm and strong, sent a shiver of anticipation through her. Far from resenting such an intrusion into her physical privacy, she wanted him to go much farther. Hardly aware of what she was doing, she shifted beneath his hand, rubbing herself against it.

"Gwen," he muttered thickly. It was all he could do not to lay her down on the bed immediately, strip off her clothes and his own and plunge deep within her. The fire she lit in him was all but unbearable. He throbbed with need for her, and with an impatience he had not felt since he was a randy boy of sixteen.

"Now you're smiling," she said softly through lips that parted on a sigh.

"I was remembering how simple it used to be."

"Wham, bam, thank you, ma'am?" she teased.

He winced and laughed ruefully. "Not quite that bad, but close." His hand moved upward to capture and gently knead her breast. His eyes never left her face, drinking in her reaction. "But that was a long time ago."

She breathed in sharply. Warmth spread over her cheeks. Her eyelids drooped slightly, making her gaze slumberous.

"You like that," he said, rather than asked.

Her only response was a small, affirmative noise that could easily have been mistaken for a purr. Then she put her hands on his chest.

He caught her fingers with his and brought them to the buttons of his shirt. She hesitated, but only for a moment, before swiftly undoing them. Her hands slipped past the open edges to touch his heated skin.

Owen jerked with the shock of her caress, simple as it was. He saw her catch her lower lip between her teeth but it was as though things were happening in slow motion. Time seemed to become meaningless as they moved together, beginning a dance that was as ancient as humanity, yet forever new.

Gwen was still aware enough to be surprised at how quickly her natural shyness and modesty dissolved with him. It seemed the most natural thing in the world when he lowered her gown until her breasts were fully bared to both his eyes and hands. As the cool air touched her, she trembled slightly, but that turned quickly to tremors of passion as he lowered his head and touched her gently with his lips.

Tenderly he lifted each breast to his mouth, licking and suckling her gently until both nipples were glistening and hard with desire. "Look," he whispered. "Look at how beautiful you are."

She obeyed and was jolted by the sight. He was liberating her in some way she had never experienced before, cutting bonds that had kept her from soaring free.

And soar she did when he lowered her onto the bed and came down beside her, his mouth suddenly voracious on hers, his tongue driving deeply as his hands twisted in her hair to hold her still.

Gwen writhed beneath him, her arms clinging across his broad back. The nightgown rode up, exposing her bare legs to the rough denim of his jeans. Smooth and rough, silk and steel, gentleness and demand, the contrast of sensations all but overwhelmed her.

She closed her eyes and saw the darkness behind her lids whirl. The air was cool against her skin. His clean breath clung to her. His skin tasted of musk and sweat, the salty tang of a fully aroused male. She was fast sinking into a vortex of passion, losing herself in him and finding delight in the yielding.

Owen was gripped by pleasure no less intense. He wanted to savor every inch of her, but he didn't know if he could hold out much longer against her innate seductiveness. The corded muscles of his arms clenched as he held himself above her, looking down into the perfection of a face flushed with pleasure and something more: sheer delight.

"I never..." she breathed softly. "You make me feel..."

"I know," he whispered, lowering only his head to flick his tongue across the crest of her breast. "I've never felt anything like this, either."

It was true; for all the women he had bedded, he came to her feeling fresh and new. Perhaps it was the long period of celibacy that had preceded their meeting, or simply the emotions she aroused, but she made him believe that anything a man could dream could become reality.

She had spread the edges of his shirt farther apart, giving her access to the broad expanse of tanned skin. Small male nipples nestled in whorls of dark hair. Driven to give him the same pleasure he was giving her, she touched her mouth to him lightly.

Owen gasped. He threw his head back, his eyes closed, and savored the sensations rippling through him. Emboldened by his response, Gwen went farther, licking and biting him gently.

He bore it as long as he could, then rolled over abruptly onto his side, carrying her with him. "Enough. You'll have me bursting."

A languid, female smile spread across her features. "Really?"

"Witch, you know what you're doing to me."

Yet she didn't, not really. But the learning delighted her. He saw the anticipation that prompted her to reach out for him again and laughed. "Give me a minute."

"Why?" she demanded artlessly.

"For this." He levered himself away from her and stood beside the bed, quickly shucking his clothes. His hands trembled at the waistband of his jeans, but he managed to get the zipper down and pull them off. All the while she watched him with unabashed fascination. In the moonlight his body was all shadowed planes and silvered angles. He looked like a magnificent statue, hammered and chiseled by a master sculptor. He was also undeniably, proudly male.

Gwen sat up on the bed, her legs folded under her, the nightgown drifting around her waist. She put her arms around his slender hips and-leaned her head against his flat belly. Her eyes fluttered shut languorously as she traced with her lips and tongue the line of hair that arched across his abdomen.

Her own daring astounded her, but whatever hesitation she might have felt was burned away by the urgency of her need to know him. She could not remain passive in this, their first experience of love. All her inborn feminine power demanded that she give as well as receive.

His manhood arched hot and heavy into her welcoming hands. She stroked him tenderly, fascinated by his silken power. So caught up was she in the sheer beauty of him that she lost track of what she was doing to him, until a hoarse cry broke from him at the same moment he caught her head between his large palms and pulled her back.

"Enough." His face was set in hard, implacable lines; his eyes glittered with absolute determination. He had reached the limits of his restraint and could wait no longer.

His body was heavy and demanding on hers as he lowered her again onto the bed. This time he let her feel all his weight and strength just long enough to make her gasp softly. Then he lifted himself up and proceeded to torment her as delightfully as she had him.

Their bodies glistened with sweat as they strained together. Once, only once, Gwen tried to stop him, stunned by the daring of his caress, but he grasped her wrists in one large hand and continued to do as he wished, and, indeed, as she also desired.

Fire licked through her veins; a pool of heat grew in her belly; her breasts burned, and between her parted thighs a soft, moist excitement burgeoned.

He filled her with a single, powerful stroke that wrung a high cry from her, not of pain, but of sheer fulfillment. For a moment he remained still within her, letting her become accustomed to his size and strength. Then her legs wrapped more tightly around him, and her hips rose, drawing him deeper. Together they moved to the ancient rhythms, pulses of the moon and tides, currents that carried them farther and farther into a roiling sea until they were at last tossed up like shipwrecked survivors on a golden shore, where they clung together, sated and reborn.

So it was throughout the glittering night. They slept only briefly, waking to find themselves caught once again in the storm of their own making. Secret fantasies, half-imagined joys, supreme sensations, were all within their reach. They held nothing back, finding in each other the missing part of themselves.

Which should not have been possible, Gwen thought as she studied Owen in the slowly gathering light. What did she know about him, really, except that he was a man of rare imagination and determination who possessed a kind of strength she had never encountered before? Like it or not, she had clearly decided at some point to do as he asked and trust him. So far she had no indication that she had made a mistake, yet in the aftermath of what they had shared, she couldn't help but be apprehensive. She was so vulnerable now; all her defenses were stripped away. He knew her to a degree no one else ever had, perhaps not even herself.

But, then, she reminded herself, she also knew him. Not in the way of facts and figures, life stories, but in the way that the heart sensed what truly lay beneath the surface.

That comforted her, and she laid her head down again on his chest, feeling the rhythmic rise and fall of his breathing. Not until his hand stroked down the length of her back to cup her buttocks did she realize that he, too, was awake.

"Good morning," he murmured, touching his lips to her brow.

"Hmmm, morning."

"Tired?"

"Exhausted, but somehow..."

"I know," he said, and she felt the laughter in his throat. "It doesn't seem to matter."

"We must be crazy. People can die from this."

"But what a way to go."

They laughed together, almost giddily, as though that were the funniest thing they had ever heard. Somehow, in the midst of the laughter, he moved, or she did, and they were caught again, entwined in passion.

Much later, when full morning light was streaming through the windows, they at last left the bed. Gwen winced slightly as she stood up, and Owen was instantly concerned. "Are you all right?" he asked, drawing her close.

She nodded, but wryly. "Why is it I suddenly feel a bit bowlegged?"

"Can't imagine," he assured her, deadpan. But he insisted on scooping her up and carrying her into the bathroom, despite her halfhearted protests.

The shower mustered its usual desultory stream of tepid water, but neither of them minded. In the narrow cubicle they soaped each other leisurely, cupping handfuls of water to rinse. It was a very, very long shower, and during it Gwen discovered that certain things she would have thought physically impossible were instead quite achievable, not to mention immensely enjoyable.

She had no clear memory of turning off the water or leaving the shower, except that she knew Owen wrapped her in a towel and carried her back into the bedroom. They tumbled, wet and weary, across the sheets and slept again, until hunger of a different kind finally roused them.

With a fine disregard for their digestive systems, they raided the refrigerator. Owen assembled a truly impressive hero sandwich for them to share, while Gwen put together a salad. They opened a bottle of white wine and enjoyed the impromptu meal in companionable silence until the worst pangs of hunger were satisfied. Then they turned playful, feeding each other choice bits interspersed with kisses.

"I could get very used to this," Owen murmured when they were finally at the sink washing up the dishes. The simple domesticity surrounding them meant a great deal to him. It was an ingredient never before present in his relationships with women, and that he had introduced into his own life only with considerable effort. For so long he had been footloose, if not fancy-free. With some surprise he realized how intensely he disliked the idea of ever returning to that kind of existence.

Yet he might not have any choice, unless he could persuade her to stay. If she left, the pleasure he found in the part of the world he considered home would go with her.

"Gwen," he said, wiping his hands on the dish towel, "I have to go back to the monastery to feed Lancelot and the others. Come with me?"

The tension that had seeped into him had not yet touched her. She smiled radiantly and glanced down at them both with a teasing light in her eyes. "Of course, but I think we should put some clothes on first."

Her easy acceptance reassured him, and he was able to join in her amusement. "I suppose it might startle someone to see us roaming around so...informally."

''Hmmm, not to mention that we'd probably catch a chill.''

''Funny you should mention that,'' he said, leaning closer to lightly nuzzle her throat. ''You've got goose bumps already.''

''So,'' she informed him, her hands stroking down his back to his firm buttocks, ''do you.''

''Better go upstairs, then, and get warmed up.''

''All that way?'' She glanced meaningfully toward the sitting room, which, after all, was much closer.

The old couch there might not be the most comfortable, but neither of them noticed as they put it to good use. So enthralled were they that the ringing telephone went unnoticed and died away long before they surfaced again from the dizzying vortex of their own delight.

Chapter 10

After they had given Lancelot his dinner and put feed out for the sheep and chickens, they stopped by the stable. Alexander and three other falcons sat on perches near the entrance. They bobbed their heads at Owen and suffered him to scratch their breast feathers before he put out food for them.

Gwen took one glance at the ground delicacy and looked away, preferring not to inquire what it was. Owen caught her discomfort and grinned. "Don't worry. Most days they hunt."

"I guess I'm just not used to so much...nature."

"It does have a rough as well as a beautiful side," he admitted. "But at least a death that sustains life isn't in vain."

He had a point there. So much violence served no purpose at all, except to vent anger and hatred. Whatever rationalizations people applied to acts of cruelty always rang hollow. She thought of the headline she had seen about the bombing in Cardiff and had to fight against a wave of depression. All her emotions were primed and vulnerable; she felt everything more intensely, and was at once frightened and elated by that.

Wind Dancer was in the paddock beyond the stable. Owen took a halter from the wall where the well-polished tack hung and went out to him. For a moment the magnificent stallion pretended to ignore him, but then both training and affection won through.

Gwen caught her breath as she watched the horse race at full stride toward the man who stood waiting for him. His immense hooves tore up great clods of earth as his chestnut mane rippled in the sun. Owen didn't move a muscle, simply waiting calmly in the direct path of the great animal.

Wind Dancer was almost upon him, when he stopped suddenly, whinnied and stuck his muzzle out to be petted. Gwen couldn't hear what Owen murmured to him, but it seemed to satisfy the stallion, who allowed the halter to be slipped on before he was led back into the stable.

"He's incredibly beautiful," Gwen said reverently as man and horse joined her. She shied away from them slightly, respecting Wind Dancer far too much not to give him a wide berth. The horse in turn eyed her with watchful curiosity that suggested she was being carefully weighed in the balance.

"He's also something of a fake," Owen said with a laugh. "You won't find a horse who can look more ferocious, but underneath he's pure mush."

"I'll take your word for it," Gwen murmured.

"You can do better than that. Here." He held out a carrot to her, which immediately caught Wind Dancer's attention. "Go ahead, feed him."

"Uh, I don't really think . . ."

As it turned out, she had no choice. While she was still debating what to do, the stallion lowered his head, delicately nipped the carrot from between her fingers, devoured it in a single crunch and proceeded to lick her hand.

"Oh," Gwen said, breaking into giggles. "That tickles."

Owen smiled at them both. "See what I mean. A fake."

"A sweet one." Emboldened, she scratched the great horse behind his ear, which won her a look of such devotion that she burst out laughing. "So much for my fear of horses."

"I'll have you riding in no time," Owen said confidently. And with a bit of luck he would also have her feeling so completely at home that she would never want to go back to the States.

Before leaving Myrddin's Rock he had suggested that she bring a few things along and plan to stay the night. Gwen had agreed readily enough simply because she saw no reason to be hypocritical; she wanted to be with him every bit as much as he wanted to be with her. But once they had the animals settled down and were returning to the house she began to feel rather shy. It was one thing to surrender to passion on the spur of the moment; it was quite another to deliberately plan for it.

Owen sensed her unease and moved swiftly to soothe it. He showed her around the part of the building that she hadn't yet seen, including those parts that had not yet been restored, explaining as they went all that he planned to do.

"It will take years, of course," he admitted when they had made their way back to the entry hall. "But it has to be done slowly to be done right."

"I can see that," Gwen said. "What you've finished so far is magnificent." She wasn't flattering him; her curator's eye fully appreciated the meticulousness of his restoration. Beneath his hands ancient walls were coming once again to life. They paused before a large tapestry depicting the birth of the Christ child. Gwen had noticed it before, but hadn't looked at it closely. She did so now, and her lips parted on a silent note of wonder.

"This is an original," she said, reaching out a hand, but stopping short of touching the beautifully faded cloth.

Owen nodded. "It dates from the fourteenth century. Though I have no reason to believe it belonged to the monastery, it is the sort of ornament the good brothers would have allowed themselves.

"But it—" She broke off, not wanting to be so crass as to point out what he must already know, that the tapestry was worth a fortune. She had purchased several similar pieces for the museum and knew their worth.

"There's another in the bedroom," Owen said. "If you'd care to see it."

She did, not the least because her curiosity was well and truly caught. She had presumed that while Owen was hardly as impecunious as Daniel had tried to suggest, he was doing the work on the house himself in order to save money. Now she had to wonder if it wasn't more a case of simply enjoying himself. The tapestry suggested a substantial income, at odds with what appeared to be a life well removed from the materialistic rat race.

If the tapestry in the entry hall had threatened to take her breath away, the one in the bedroom did so for certain. More worldly in theme, it depicted a beautiful maiden seated in the entrance of a tournament tent, observing the clash of two armored knights, who appeared to be vying for her hand.

Across from it, dominating the large room, was an elaborately carved bed, complete with embroidered hangings. Gracefully curved stools, an ironbound chest and a handwoven rug completed the furnishings. From the high ceiling crisscrossed by age-darkened beams hung a wrought-iron chandelier similar in design to a partially completed one Gwen had seen in the blacksmith shed.

"I got a little carried away here," Owen explained. "The monks lived very simply in dormitories curtained off into cubicles with simple wooden beds and straw-filled mattresses. They followed the Benedictine rule here, rising several times throughout the night to pray. Their meals were extremely simple, and they practiced frugality in everything they did." He smiled faintly. "I can only hope none of them are turning over in their graves now that I'm in residence."

"I suspect they would have understood," Gwen murmured. "After all, some of them must have been experienced men before they came here and closed themselves off from the world."

"Undoubtedly, but as for closing themselves off..." He shook his head. "If that was their goal, they failed. The world intruded again and again. Finally it destroyed them."

"What happened?" Gwen asked, sitting down on the edge of the bed.

"Henry VIII and the Reformation."

Gwen nooded, thinking of that terrible time when, in order to divorce the wife who couldn't give him sons, old Henry founded a new faith and in the process seized religious property throughout his kingdom. Priests, friars, monks and nuns were all dispossessed, literally put out on the road to starve.

"This place," Owen explained, "managed to hold out a little longer by virtue of its remote location, but finally it, too, fell."

"My family," Gwen said thoughtfully, "the Llywelyns, did they have any part to play in those events?"

"Only to try to stave them off. They had suffered a great deal themselves under the English rule, but had retained enough authority to still be considered the natural leaders of the people here. According to documents I've seen, many of that last group of monks found shelter at Myrddin's Rock, at least until other arrangements could be made."

"It sounds as though you've researched it all very carefully," Gwen said.

He shrugged. "I suppose you could say it's more than a hobby, but not quite a vocation. I've found something here that always eluded me before, a place to put down roots."

"So many people are afraid of that these days."

He nodded, coming to stand before her. "Because they don't want to commit themselves to anything, or anyone."

She didn't have to be told that Owen was different. He was a man who thrived on commitments, to his homeland, to his vision of past glories and his determination to bring them alive for the present and the future.

But that wasn't quite the same thing as making a commitment to another person. She knew from her own experience how very difficult it was to reach out to someone else on any but the most safely superficial level.

"Owen," she said nervously, looking down at her hands, "I just want you to know that I don't expect anything from you."

He stopped in the midst of reaching out to touch her shoulders. "What are you talking about?"

"Only that what happened last night doesn't mean we owe each other anything."

"Owe? What on earth does that have to do with it? When did we start to talk about debts?"

"That's what I'm trying to say." And not making a very good job of it, she thought. A quick glance up at him revealed such stormy anger darkening his face that she looked away again hastily. "We shouldn't try to read too much into it."

"Are you saying," he demanded, "that it didn't mean anything to you?"

"No, of course not." Now it was her turn to get angry; he seemed to be deliberately misunderstanding her. But before she could say so, he went on fiercely.

"I suppose you make love like that with whatever man happens to catch your eye."

"I most certainly do not! Where do you get off even suggesting such a thing?"

"I didn't suggest it. You did, by pretending that what we shared is of no consequence. I'd forgotten how artfully casual everything is in the States," he continued contemptuously. "Heaven forbid anyone should feel an honest emotion beyond simple lust. Well, if that's all you want, fine with me. I'm just the man for you.''

As he spoke, he was unbuttoning his shirt. It landed in a heap at his feet as his hands went to the waistband of his jeans. "Forget making love. That's for sentimental idiots. Let's have sex, or is that still too euphemistic for you? How about a nice—"

"Stop it," she exclaimed, scrambling to the far side of the bed. "You're the touchiest man. I didn't mean—"

"Touchy?" He stopped in the midst of dropping his pants and shot her an incredulous look. "That's what you call it? You tell me that the most incredibly beautiful experience of my life meant nothing to you and when I object you call me touchy?"

"If the shoe fits," she murmured, then added more placatingly, "Look, all I meant was that you shouldn't feel pressured because we went to bed together."

When he continued to stare at her stonily, Gwen's composure began to crack. It seemed as though everything had turned terribly wrong without warning, just when she wanted it to be so completely right. Tears blurred her eyes as she looked away from him. "Forget it. We're not speaking the same language."

He knelt on the mattress and leaned toward her, his big hand gently stroking her hair. "Don't be so sure of that, sweetheart. It seems to me that we can communicate just fine if we leave words out of it."

"Sooner or later," she reminded him through suddenly dry lips, "we'll have to talk."

"I agree, but maybe by then we'll understand each other better."

Certainly very few barriers were allowed to remain between them as their clothes fell away and they stretched out side by side on the big bed. Gwen had a fleeting vision of generations of long-gone monks shaking their heads over the foibles of humanity before turning discreetly away. She reassured herself that they, more than most, would understand one of the ultimate expressions of life's beauty and the Creator's love.

What she and Owen shared had nothing to do with the crude, meaningless act he had threatened. Each touch of his mouth and hands on her was reverent and awe-inspiring, raising her to new heights of incandescent joy. She explored his body as thoroughly as he did her own, finding in it a universe of perfection. When he trembled beneath her touch and gasped her name, she felt a soaring sense of her own life force matching his.

The late-afternoon light faded even as their passion lit the quiet room. A lark sang in the vines beyond the window, and far out over the beach sea gulls called. Gwen heard nothing but the beating of Owen's heart and hers and the sharp cadence of their breathing as they climbed together toward a glittering pinnacle.

When they reached it, consciousness slipped away and they fell as naturally into sleep as children who had played innocently and well beneath a benevolent sun.

Long ago, in times and places he did not care to remember, Owen had acquired the habit of needing very little sleep. He was accustomed to waking during the night and often felt that he did his best thinking then. But he was not thinking now. Rather, he was content simply to lie with his arms around Gwen, holding her in a protective embrace as he listened to the deeply running currents of instinct within him.

She was in danger. He couldn't figure out how or why, but he was convinced that the threat was real. While he had wanted her to return with him and spend the night simply because he enjoyed the sight of her in his own home, he had also considered it safest to keep her away from Myrddin's Rock until he could determine what was happening there.

Could there be anything to the legend Winny had related to him? Logically, he didn't think so. But logic did not always prevail. He had seen things he would never in his life be able to explain.

But somehow he had to come up with an explanation that would satisfy her and convince her to do as he wished. Before dawn he left the bed and padded soundlessly into the kitchen, where he fixed himself a pot of coffee and sat drinking it at the old wooden table. Lancelot had risen from his place beside the fire and laid his head companionably on Owen's knee. He scratched the dog absently as he looked out through the window at the swirling ribbons of early morning mist.

If only that call hadn't come from Cardiff. He resented the intrusion into his carefully constructed life even as he understood the need for it. The sound of Winston's voice had taken him back years to the time when he was a very different man. He couldn't go back to what he had been, no matter how great the pressure to do so.

Owen smiled grimly as he refilled his mug. Winston had sworn that no undue influence would be brought to bear. He had been perfectly safe in making that pledge, since he knew that Owen's sense of duty would compel him to cooperate. The oath he had sworn bound him as tightly now as it had on the day he took it.

He rose and stretched his long, hard body beneath the short terry-cloth robe he had put on in deference to the coolness. Years had passed since he had been called upon to do what he had once done with ease. Though he had stayed in superb shape, he wondered if his reflexes were still as sharp. Whether they were or not, he knew for a fact that he could no longer muster the same ruthlessness that had once been second nature to him.

The years had gentled him, and his encounter with Gwen had completed the process. He thought of how angry she had inadvertently made him, and smiled wryly. He was vulnerable to her in ways that no longer frightened him. Rather, his response to her filled him with hope for the future, provided he could bring it to pass.

Lancelot woofed softly at his side. He opened the door and let the dog out, then returned to the stove to fix a fresh pot of coffee. He was drinking too much of the stuff and ought to at least eat something while he was at it, but he had plans to make and needed to concentrate on them to the exclusion of all else.

That did not, however, prevent him from keeping an ear out for any sign of activity from the bedroom. The moment she began to stir, shortly after daybreak, he went in to her.

She was sleeping on her side, the sheet pushed down to her waist and her red-gold hair spread out over the pillow. Her breasts were pushed together, the nipples slightly erect.

He bent over her silently, lifting the sheet and slowly edging it down over her hips, her thighs and farther, until she was fully bared to his gaze. He stood for a long time looking down at her, thinking of the beauty of what they had shared and how extraordinarily close he felt to this woman he hadn't even met a few days before. He could easily envision many more nights such as the one they had shared, but he could also see himself living peacefully at her side, content to grow old together. Provided contrary fate would allow them to.

Gently he re-covered her, but not before dropping a feather-light kiss on the curve of her hip. The slight swell of her belly brushed his cheek. He thought of a child growing there, and his hand trembled.

He sat down on the edge of the bed and waited until she stirred again and her eyes fluttered open.

"What...?" she murmured sleepily. "Oh... Owen...."

He smiled and dropped a teasing kiss on the tip of her nose. "How nice, you remembered."

"I always did have a good memory for names." She turned over on her side and yawned. "What time is it?"

"Around seven. You could go back to sleep if you wanted."

"I'm too hungry." She stretched languidly and through half-shuttered lids threw him a boldly seductive glance. "We worked up quite an appetite."

Her audacity, overcoming what he knew to be natural reticence, delighted him. He laughed out loud, unaware of how the corded muscles of his throat worked with the sound. Gray-green eyes gone silvery followed them down to the exposed vee of his chest. She moistened her lips, feeling her nipples harden further beneath the sheet. There was a heaviness between her thighs and a seeping languor that defied her to do anything besides wait passively to see how he would react.

He bent closer, the scent of his sun-bronzed skin filling her. She felt the heat of his body seeping into her skin. Her head rose from the pillow for an instant only to fall back. Her eyes fluttered shut as he pressed his lips to the scented hollow between her collarbones.

"Hungry, are you?" he murmured.

"Hmmm." She was, but in a very different sort of way than she had been moments before.

His hand passed almost roughly over her body, touching her through the sheet with raw male possessiveness. She moaned and lifted her slender arms to embrace him. His mouth closed on hers voraciously, his tongue thrusting into her even as he yanked her sole covering away. His robe fell open, and he shrugged it off impatiently.

"I can't believe how much I want you," he gasped as his body hardened painfully. Still, he struggled to restrain himself until he was certain she was ready.

"Please," she gasped. "Don't wait."

He looked down at her, his eyes smoldering. "Are you sure?"

She nodded frantically and reached for him. Her legs parted, and she guided him into her.

As her moist heat enveloped him, his self-control broke. Kneeling between her open thighs, he drove into her hard and fast. His hands, gripping her hips, raised her so that he could plunge even more deeply. She cried out and gripped him tightly with powerful inner muscles. The possessor became the possessed as she claimed him utterly.

Tendons rippled down the length of his broad back as he loomed over her, watching intently as the first signs of release swept over her. He held back, enthralled, until she cried out and arched beneath him, her nails drawing blood as they dug into his back.

Heedless of that small hurt, he moved within her with all his strength, surrendering to the little death that heralded the renewal of life.

Chapter 11

I have to go away for a day or two," Owen said much later when they were seated at the kitchen table, sharing a postponed breakfast. The day had already turned warm, and they had the windows wide open, admitting the scent of lavender from the bushes that grew wild just beyond the door.

Up until then the meal had been a gently teasing interlude, with numerous pauses for long glances and pleasant silences. Yet Gwen had been aware of his gathering tension and had wondered at its cause.

"Why?" she asked, putting down the slice of toast she had been about to butter. She tried to sound casual, but the question came out stark and protesting.

"Business," he said, his eyes sliding away from her. "It shouldn't take long. At any rate, I'd appreciate it if you could do me a favor. Would you stay here and keep an eye on the animals for me?''

That was the excuse he had come up with for preventing her from returning alone to Myrddin's Rock. Without revealing his concern, he waited anxiously to learn if she would go for it.

"I suppose they do need to be fed, don't they?" she asked doubtfully. The only animal she had ever cared for was a friend's Persian cat, and he had been notably independent.

He nodded. "I'll show you where everything is, and," he promised with a smile, "I'll take care of the falcons before I go, so you won't have to worry about them."

It sounded simple enough, and she could hardly refuse. "All right, but I don't actually have to stay here, do I? I could come over once a day, or twice if necessary, to look after them." She didn't add that she would be far more comfortable in her own home, away from constant reminders of him that would make his absence all the more painful.

"Actually," he said, still not looking at her directly, "I'd rather you stayed. There have been some livestock thefts in the area recently. The kind of thing that crops up anywhere. I'd feel a lot more secure if I knew there was someone here the whole time I'm gone."

For a total fabrication, not to say an outright lie, he thought that sounded fairly convincing. Fortunately she had no way of knowing that such theft was unheard of on Anglesey, where people were far too aware of each other's movements for anyone to get away with such a crime.

"I see," she said, her brow furrowing. In her growing fascination with the island she had managed to lose sight of the fact that the outside world must occasionally intrude. "Is it Wind Dancer you're worried about?"

Owen shrugged in what he hoped was a noncommittal fashion. "There's no doubt he'd be a great temptation, but I'd hate to lose any of them. They're almost like family."

Having appealed to her on such a fundamental level, he didn't think she would be able to refuse. Nor was he disappointed.

"All right," she said at length. "I'll stay, but I'll have to go home first for some clothes."

He thought she looked just fine in what she had on, a thin silk robe that clung to her lovingly, but he resisted saying so. Though she made no attempt to move away, he could feel her withdrawing from him. The loving, intimate mood of the night before was fading. He hated to see it go, even though he couldn't blame her for becoming cautious. So much had happened between them so quickly that second thoughts were inevitable.

If only he didn't have to leave. Silently he cursed the duty that demanded he go, while struggling to keep his expression reassuring. "Is there anything you'd like me to pick up for you in Cardiff?"

She shook her head. "No, I've got everything I need."

"I'll leave a number where you can reach me, if something should come up." Or at least through which a message could be gotten to him.

She brushed that aside. "I'm sure everything will be fine."

Her determined self-reliance irked him, but he made no comment. It was enough, for the moment, that she had agreed to stay.

They returned to Myrddin's Rock together, despite Gwen's protests that she could manage alone. Owen didn't mention that he wanted to get another look at the staircase and the power lines. The utility company had been notified and had promised to send someone out.

While Gwen packed a small suitcase he checked the steps leading to the pantry again. He found no further evidence that her accident had been deliberately caused, but neither did he see anything to indicate the contrary. If someone had done it, as he was still instinctively inclined to think, they were good at their work.

Which worried him all the more. He was frowning when she rejoined him in the kitchen. "Is something wrong?" she asked, putting her bag down.

"What? Oh, no, I was just thinking that with the power out, it's as well that you aren't staying here."

"I'll check in tomorrow to see how things are," she said, glancing around to make sure she hadn't forgotten anything. The kitchen had changed subtly during her days of occupancy. A handful of heather that she had picked on the hillside and put in an old brown crock added color to the window over the sink. She had turned over the handwoven rug under the table to reveal brilliant reds and greens, hidden for years from the sun. Perhaps the next time she was in the village she would pick up some new place mats and napkins.

"Why don't you wait until I come back?" Owen suggested watching her gray-green eyes move around the room and hoping that he was right about what he saw in them. "After all, there's nothing really urgent here, is there?"

"No," she admitted, "I suppose not." She didn't feel ready to admit how important Myrddin's Rock was becoming to her. While it was hardly the most comfortable place to live—not in any way comparable to Owen's home—there was something about it that drew her. More and more she hated the idea of it passing into the hands of strangers.

They were in the car when they heard the muted ring of the telephone. Gwen's hand paused on the ignition key. "Darn it, by the time I get there, whoever it is will have hung up."

"Forget it. They'll call back another time."

"I suppose." She hesitated a moment, then shrugged. "It's probably a wrong number. Hardly anyone would be trying to reach me here." Offhand, the only person she could think of who might be calling was Daniel, and she didn't particularly want to talk with him in front of Owen, not with the animosity between the two men as strong as it was.

Back at the monastery Owen showed her where all the feed was and what to do with it. Lancelot trailed along at their heels, intently watching every move they made. When Owen took the falcons out to hunt, the dog remained with Gwen, trotting after her into the bedroom when she unpacked. She had briefly considered using the small guest room she'd noticed off one of the corridors, but rejected that idea. She was still wary but she was also honest enough to admit that there was no turning back from the direction their relationship had taken.

"Going to keep me company, boy?" she asked Lancelot as she put away her belongings in the oak chest against the whitewashed wall, beneath the mullioned windows.

He sat on his haunches, his head tilted to one side, and looked from her to the foot of the bed with genuine hopefulness.

Gwen laughed and patted him on the head. Owen came in as she was doing so and smiled at the scene. "I won't have to worry about your being well protected.

"Are they, uh, fed?" she asked.

"Amply. They'll be fine until I get back." He undid his shirt as he spoke and stripped it off. "I'm going to get a shower and change."

Such casual domesticity made her flush. He saw her discomfort, and his smile widened. "You're welcome to join me, of course."

"No, thanks," she told him tartly. "I'm clean enough."

"I thought you were convinced the other morning that showers have other purposes."

The sight of his bare, browned chest lightly lathered with sweat from the hunt was almost enough to convince her. Only with great difficulty did she shake her head. "I wouldn't want to hold you up."

In fact, he was running late, since he was due in Cardiff early that evening. But he was so reluctant to leave her that the temptation to linger was all but irresistible. At that moment he had to be glad of the stubborn independence that sent her from the room. It was all that enabled him to keep his mind on business.

Even so, he turned the shower all the way to cold and stood under it for long minutes, not because he really believed that had any effect on sexual potency—his was certainly defiantly resilient—but because the biting spray at least helped to clear his head.

Afterward he shaved again and dressed in a dark gray suit the *cognoscenti* would have recognized as originating on Savile Row. With it he wore a blue, custom-tailored shirt of Egyptian cotton and a regimental silk tie, which, unlike so many men who affected such things, he actually had the right to don.

A quick glance in the mirror as he fastened the Windsor knot showed him a man he hadn't seen in quite some time: urbane, successful, a hunter in the caverns where power and wealth lurked. He fastened a thin gold watch around his left wrist, picked up a black calfskin overnight bag and left the room.

Gwen was in the inner courtyard, staring pensively at the fountain where starlings and finches came to drink. She sat on a stone bench a short distance away, her pose unconsciously graceful and utterly feminine. Her back was straight, her breasts raised; one hand brushed absently at a spray of larkspur growing nearby.

She turned as the gravel crunched under his feet, and he saw the look of surprise that darted across her features. "Owen...?"

"You look very much at home here," he said softly.

The breeze blew a strand of her red-gold hair across her brow. He brushed it away gently and let his hand drift down over her smooth cheek to cup her chin. "I'm glad you agreed to stay."

Gwen stared up at the tall, powerfully built man who touched her so tenderly. It was the same man she had slept beside the night before, the same one who had become her lover with such devastating thoroughness, but he was also startlingly different.

"I have to go," he said quickly before she could voice the confusion that was so clearly in her mind.

"If I'm not back by tomorrow, I will be the day after."

He dropped a light kiss on her upturned mouth, gave her what he hoped was a reassuring smile and strode quickly out of the garden. Gwen was left staring after him, pale and bemused.

"Well," she said when he was gone, "there's food for thought." Lancelot looked up from where he had positioned himself by her feet the moment Owen departed. "When your master gets back," she told him, "he and I are going to have a little chat. I've got the definite feeling I'm missing something here."

That feeling persisted, growing into conviction, as she deliberately made herself at home. Puttering around the garden, she found a bed of fresh herbs and decided on the spur of the moment to attempt a fairly ambitious dinner, which, if nothing else, would have the virtue of keeping her preoccupied for some time.

A quick glance around the kitchen confirmed that Owen's culinary skills did not come from cookbooks, unless he kept them in his den. She looked in there, not intending to let herself be distracted, but was caught by the cool, quiet room crowded with books. Remembering that she would need something to read that night, since she was realistic enough to expect sleep to be elusive, she chose a favorite volume by James Owens and was turning to leave, when her eye fell on the pile of papers on the desk.

The words neatly typed on the top page jumped out at her: "The Impact of Deforestation on the Indigenous Population of North Wales circa 1750 by James Owens.''

Heavy stuff, not exactly what editors were lining up to buy as the next bestseller, but perfectly in tone with the monographs published in the more respected academic quarterlies. Owens had written his share of those, was in fact always in demand for them, in between his more popular works.

Which did not explain what the article was doing there on Owen's desk. Unless, of course, one accepted the obvious explanation.

It was never pleasant to have one's obtuseness starkly revealed. Gwen sat down heavily in the chair nearest the desk and stared at the stack of papers as though it were a viper arched to strike at her.

Why hadn't she guessed? Owen's devotion to Welsh history, his intelligence and articulateness, even his mysterious affluence, all pointed in the same direction as James Owens's writings. She flipped to the back of the book she had chosen and stared at the place where an author's photo would normally have appeared.

Nothing, except for a brief biography that gave only sketchy professional credentials. If she remembered correctly, Owens's photo never appeared on any of his books, but the biography cited for him was so full of achievements as to suggest that he was an older man laden with years as well as honors.

Why the deception? What purpose could it possibly serve for Owen to hide his true identity, if indeed she was correct about who he really was? While it was true that he would undoubtedly have attracted some attention from his neighbors, since the Welsh nurtured a deeply rooted love of the scholarly and the literary, surely his privacy would still have been respected.

A tantalizingly vague answer flitted through the back of her mind, something she had heard at one time and remembered, but not clearly enough to consciously recall now. Something to do with James Owens and why he might choose to live under a different name. Try as she did, she couldn't catch the wavering thread of memory. Finally she gave up in frustration.

"Come on, boy," she said to Lancelot as she started back to the kitchen. There was a leg of lamb in the refrigerator large enough to feed six. Deciding that if Owen—or James—had been saving it for something he should have said so, she rubbed it with olive oil and garlic, spread sprigs of fresh rosemary on top and put it in the oven, along with handfuls of potatoes and carrots.

The meal was the sort she associated with Sunday dinner as a child, and it would feed her for several days, even with generous scraps for Lancelot. Which was just as well, since the more she thought of Owen's deception, the less she felt inclined to do anything so calming as cook.

"Your master is going to have to answer some tough questions when he gets back," she told the dog as they went out to feed the other animals. He woofed his encouragement while she poured oats and fresh water for Wind Dancer, tossed corn meal to the chickens and took care of the rest. By the time she was done a cooling breeze had sprung up, and it was getting on to evening.

The delectable aroma of roast lamb filled the kitchen when she returned. She washed her hands at the stone sink, gave Lancelot his dinner and was setting the table, when the phone rang.

She answered it to silence, followed by the stiff clearing of a throat.

"Gwen..." Daniel said. "I've been trying to reach you."

The suggestion of censure in his voice made her grin wryly. She could just imagine what he was thinking, and this time he was right. Nonetheless, she took great pleasure in saying, "Owen's gone to Cardiff. He asked me to house-sit for him."

"House-sit...?"

"To stay over to look after the animals. He's worried about the thieves."

"Thieves?"

Was Daniel going to repeat everything she said? If so, the conversation would get very tedious very quickly. Briskly she asked, "Was there something you called for?"

"I've been trying to reach you since yesterday. When I still couldn't get an answer I thought Owen might know where you were." Again that hint of chagrin, as though she should have had the courtesy to keep him informed of her whereabouts.

"I'm sorry," she said, though she was anything but. "Was it anything urgent?"

"Only an offer on Myrddin's Rock," he said. "A very generous one, which I think you should respond to promptly."

"I told you I was no longer sure about selling."

"So you did, but when you hear the offer I think you'll reconsider." He named a figure that had her eyebrows shooting up.

"You're not serious?" she said.

"They did start out lower," he told her, "but I bargained them up."

"You must have. That's an incredible amount of money for a rundown castle of no particular interest. Who on earth would want to pay it?"

"It's a condition of the sale that the buyer remain anonymous, but I *can* tell you that I've checked him out and everything's on the up and up."

"Anonymous?" It was her turn to repeat his words. "Isn't that unusual?"

"It happens, especially with wealthy people. There's nothing to be concerned about."

"Even so," she said thoughtfully, "I can't imagine why anyone would want to spend so much."

She thought she heard a sigh of impatience from Daniel, but he stifled it quickly and said, "Don't you have an expression in America? Don't look a gift horse in the mouth? I'd advise you to follow that recommendation here.''

''Then you think I should accept the offer?''

''Absolutely. You'd have to be crazy to turn down that much money.''

Then perhaps she was, because she was definitely thinking of refusing it. The growing conviction startled her at least as much as it would have surprised Daniel, had she mentioned it to him. When she had begun considering whether she might keep Myrddin's Rock, she'd had only a vague idea of how much it might be worth and had no qualms about forgoing the amount. But now that at least one—albeit anonymous—bidder had offered far more, she supposed she should at least give his offer serious consideration.

''I'll have to sleep on it,'' she told Daniel. ''It's too big a decision to make this instant.''

''All right,'' he said grudgingly. ''But I can't hold them off very long. They're anxious for a deal.''

And so was he, though she couldn't say exactly why. There would be a commission for him, of course, but he had already made it clear that that wasn't a major consideration. His eagerness to win her approval seemed to go beyond mere money.

''Are you in such a hurry to get rid of me?'' she teased.

There was a moment's silence before she heard the hiss of his indrawn breath. ''Of course not. It's merely that . . . this would be very good for you. If there was

some way you could get the money and still stay on I'd
be delighted.''

The words rang oddly hollow. Gwen was willing to
believe that Daniel had enjoyed her company, though
he had also resented her growing friendship with
Owen. But he was anxious for her to leave, no matter
what he said.

''Never mind,'' she murmured. ''I'll think about it
tonight and give you a call in the morning.''

''Whatever you decide?''

''Yes, of course.'' As an afterthought she added,
''Though it would be easier if I knew who made the
offer.''

''I'm sorry but I really can't tell you.''

''All right, then.''

She hung up a few moments later and sat looking at
the wall. It really was a lot of money. She could do a
great deal with it. Buy a bigger place in Cambridge.
Travel. Enjoy herself. Which presumed that she would
be returning to the States. If she stayed where she was,
the money would be of far less consequence, given
what she suspected about Owen's financial state.

But she was getting ahead of herself, thinking that
their relationship might ripen into marriage when
nothing at all had been said of that. Besides, the
pleasant, rewarding life she had enjoyed up to the
present had not become hers because she'd wanted a
man to take care of her. On the contrary, she had
achieved it on her own and in the process learned to
value her independence.

All of which gave her an excellent reason for making the decision about Myrddin's Rock alone, without interference from either Owen or Daniel.

"Dinner, Lancelot," she said firmly. "Then early to bed. I've got some heavy-duty thinking to do."

An hour later, when she had finished what turned out to be an excellent meal, she went around the house locking up, as Owen had made her promise she would.

A fog was rising off the sea, but despite it she could see a full moon riding low in the sky. A damp breeze had sprung up that made her shiver. She felt a rush of yearning inside, wishing that Owen were there to hold her.

"None of that," she murmured as she climbed the short flight of stairs to the bedroom. There would be time enough when she had straightened out a few things. Who he was, for instance. He could answer that one before she got all warm and gooey again.

And, in the meantime, she had plans of her own to make.

Chapter 12

The rumbling woke her. She was sound asleep in
Owen's bed, snug under a soft blanket and dreaming
of floating down a river with him on a sunlit day, when
the vision in the dream suddenly tilted out of control
and a great rushing sound dragged her back to consciousness.

So powerful was the tremor that she was holding on
to the edge of the bed even as she opened her eyes and
looked around apprehensively. Nothing in the room
moved; there was no outward sign of any distur-
bance, only the feeling that the very underpinnings of
her existence were crumbling.

At the foot of the bed, where he had been stretched
out asleep, Lancelot raised his head and growled
softly. "It's all right, boy," she said automatically as

she slipped from the bed and hurried over to the windows.

Nothing. The night looked utterly peaceful, if wreathed in fog. The moon had climbed, and its silvery light turned the misty ground cover to a shimmering veil.

The rumbling died away, and after a moment she wondered if she could have imagined it. Lacking any physical evidence that it had actually occurred, doubts were inevitable. And yet she couldn't shake the feeling that something had been reaching out to her, demanding her attention.

Absurd. In another moment she would be thinking that the dragon himself had called to her. "I'm sleepy," she murmured, not unlike a cranky child. "Leave me alone."

Perhaps it heard her, because it was quiet for the remainder of the night, and she didn't wake again until sunlight streamed into the room and coaxed the heaviness from her eyelids.

The fog was gone and the day bright. She stepped from the bed eagerly, a sense of adventure spurring her on. She had promised Owen that she wouldn't return to Myrddin's Rock without him, but that didn't mean she couldn't go exploring on her own.

After a quick shower, during which she couldn't help but notice that Owen's plumbing worked rather better than her own, she dried her hair and dressed in jeans and a soft blue work shirt. Still full from dinner the previous night, she didn't bother with breakfast and made quick work of feeding the animals.

With Lancelot at her heels she set out for an amble that had the virtue of being aimed in no particular direction and turned toward no particular goal. Some people couldn't do that; they had to have an objective in mind before they could even set out. But Gwen, made of sturdier stuff, was content merely to wander.

Still, she wasn't surprised when her perambulations eventually took her in the direction of the beach Owen had introduced her to. She followed the narrow pathway down to the sand, where she took off her shoes and walked along at the water's edge, playing tag with the tide.

It wasn't yet all the way in, but, even so, she had less space to walk than before. Above her rose the cliffs where the cave was hidden. Since she had no intention of venturing in there alone, she turned around and whistled for Lancelot to follow while there was still no difficulty retracing her steps.

Coming back up the pathway, holding on to the gorse bushes to pull herself along the steeper parts, she noticed for the first time that the path had been slightly widened. More sea grass and bushes were trampled down, as though several people had passed in a hurry or, alternatively, that they had been dragging something large.

When she attained the top of the cliff again she turned and looked back, noticing as she did so that a faint track showed in the sand, again giving the impression that something big had been dragged along. In another few minutes it would be obscured by the incoming tide. Wavelets were already washing up that far, blurring the lines she thought she saw enough to make her wonder if she wasn't imagining it all.

"Silly," she murmured under her breath. "What would the point be of dragging something along there? Unless, of course," she added, smiling down at Lancelot, "it was an extralarge picnic hamper."

He woofed in agreement, but an instant later set off chasing something that rustled in the bracken, and she returned to the main road to wait until he lost interest.

She was strolling along, kicking a pebble with her shoe, when the sound of an approaching car caused her to turn around. Lancelot returned at the same time, and together they watched as Daniel drew to a stop beside them.

"Just the person I was looking for," he said amiably. "Hop in and I'll give you a ride."

"All right," she said, though she really would have preferred to walk. If nothing else, she owed Daniel simple courtesy.

"Come on, boy," she said, holding the back door open for Lancelot. He held back, showing no inclination to enter the car. She finally had to take hold of his collar and push him in. Once there he emitted a low, throaty growl and dropped his head on his paws in a posture of resigned suffering.

"What's wrong with the mutt?" Daniel asked as they started off.

Gwen shrugged. "I guess he isn't feeling sociable." Actually, she was surprised by the dog's behavior; so far as she knew, he had no reason to dislike the lawyer.

"I was planning to call you later in the day," she said as they neared the old monastery. "I've been thinking about the offer."

"Before you tell me your decision, let me say that I heard again from the prospective purchasers, and they are very interested in coming to terms. I think it's possible they might even go up slightly in price."

"It's very tempting," Gwen admitted. "I could do a great deal with the money."

"Then you'll take it?" he asked eagerly.

"It's not that simple. I feel a real sense of responsibility to Myrddin's Rock now."

"You can't mean you'd really want to live there?"

"Probably not," she admitted. "It would take a great deal of work to make it comfortable, and even then, I think it's a bit too cut off for me to be happy there on my own."

"So why even consider keeping it?"

"It's hard to explain. When I came over here I certainly had no thought of holding on to the property. But being there only a short time has made me realize what the place means in terms of my family heritage. I can't just walk away from it without a qualm."

"Plenty of people have," Daniel said. "There's been an enormous turnover in old properties in the past few years."

"I'm sure, but..."

"It's Owen, isn't it? He's the one who's trying to convince you not to sell."

"He has made his feelings clear," she admitted. "But the decision is strictly my own." She wished he wouldn't bring Owen into it; that struck too close to the heart of her quandary.

"I wouldn't have thought you were the kind of woman to be influenced by such a man."

Gwen bristled. Daniel had ignored what she'd said, dismissing the fact that she was making up her own mind as though she were no more capable of doing that than a very small child. "Look," she said stiffly, "I'm not going to be browbeaten into anything, by anyone. Not you or Owen. I'll do what seems best to me. Do you understand?"

His hands had tightened on the wheel until his knuckles gleamed whitely. A pulse leaped in his jaw as he fought to suppress his anger. "The problem is," he said, "this offer isn't going to stand forever. You have to make up your mind now."

"If the offer is serious, it's not going to be withdrawn so quickly."

"It's been made very clear to me that the buyer won't wait."

"Why not?" she demanded. "After all these hundreds of years, Myrddin's Rock isn't going anywhere. What's the problem in waiting a few weeks, or even months?''

He turned onto the road leading to the monastery and slowed down slightly, giving her a sidelong look. ''I would imagine the buyer is also interested in other properties and will decide on one of them unless you accept quickly.''

''That's a risk I'll have to take,'' she insisted.

Daniel was not a man who gave up easily; moreover, he had been trained in the tough discipline of courtroom interrogation. On quiet Anglesey, he'd grown out of practice but that didn't mean he had forgotten how it was done.

''Why?'' he demanded. ''Why take the risk at all? You can walk away free and clear, with enough money to live comfortably for years.''

Put that way, she had to admit that her reluctance must seem odd. ''I can't explain it,'' she admitted, ''except to say that there's more involved here than simply stone and mortar. I have a heritage to protect. I'm the last of the Llywelyns, and I have to live up to the trust Winny put in me, at least to the extent of making sure that, whatever happens to Myrddin's Rock, its past will be protected.''

Daniel sighed deeply. She was turning out to be far more stubborn than he could have imagined. In the back of his mind he'd thought that anyone—but especially an American, from that most materialistic of cultures—would have jumped at the offer.

Heaven knew it had been tough enough to arrange, with plenty of objections raised along the way. And it wasn't going to stand much longer, no matter what she thought. The whole point of spending that much money was to get her out quickly.

He had to make her understand that, had to get her to see reason before he lost control of the situation.

"Gwen," he murmured as they pulled up in front of the house, "let me come in and talk with you about this. I promise not to, as you said, try to browbeat you. It's only that I hate to see you lose such an extraordinary opportunity."

His tone was low and conciliatory, his smile abashed. She was tempted to agree, until she spotted the Jeep parked nearby. Barely had she noticed it than Lancelot was woofing joyously and demanding to be let out of the car.

"Owen is back," she said, rather unnecessarily, since at that moment the front doors opened and the man in question stood there, his tie undone and his jacket missing, but no less dangerous for his casual pose.

"I was wondering where you'd got to," he said quietly as she got out and walked toward him, Lancelot bounding on ahead.

Owen bent and scratched the dog's ears, but his eyes never left her, except to flick briefly to Daniel who had, with some reluctance, gotten out from behind the wheel.

"Hello, Owen," he said grudgingly. "Came across Gwen on the beach road. Gave her a ride back."

This clipped explanation received only a cursory nod. Daniel stood awkwardly for a moment or two before realizing that the master of the house wasn't about to invite him in. He flushed slightly and said, "I'll be on my way, then. Give me a call later, will you, Gwen?"

She nodded, though she had barely heard him. All her attention was focused on Owen as she wondered at the change in him. He appeared to be drawn as taut as a bowstring, every inch of his powerful body honed for instant action, and she could not imagine why. Surely Daniel didn't merit such a stance.

Owen didn't move until the lawyer had gotten back in his car and driven away. Only then did he unfold himself from beside the door frame and give her a slow, lazy smile. "I missed you."

The meaning behind those words was only too clear as his eyes swept over her appreciatively. Despite herself, Gwen blushed. In an attempt to regain at least a little ground, she said, "I didn't think you'd be back this soon."

"Is that why you invited Daniel over?"

"I didn't. He gave me a lift, but now that you mention it, I did intend to ask him in." If he was going to cast aspersions on her behavior, she didn't mind doing the same for his. Tightly she said, "It was rude of you not to."

Owen shrugged, making it clear that any such consideration was inconsequential to him. "I didn't happen to feel like company."

"Then perhaps I should go."

He frowned and laid a hand on her arm. "You know damn well that's not what I meant."

In fact, she did, but that didn't mean she objected to a little persuasion. "There are things I need to do at home."

"Home?"

"You know what I mean. Let go of me."

"No, I don't think I will."

"Owen, you're being very bossy."

He nodded agreeably as he drew her farther into the house. "You bring that out in me."

"I don't respond well to bossiness. I never have."

His smile had returned, knowing, and very masculine. "We'll see."

"How was your trip?"

"We can talk about that later."

"It's lunchtime."

"We can eat later, too."

"I'm hungry now," she protested weakly.

"Hmmm, so am I."

They had reached the bedroom. His hand slid down to hold hers, their fingers intertwined. When she seemed about to raise further objections he backed her gently against the wall and kissed her deeply.

The swift, purposeful claiming of her mouth without preliminaries declared his intention to brook no refusal. She was his; he had proven that the first time they made love, and she had acknowledged it.

But he, in equal measure, was hers. He freely admitted that. Seeing her with Daniel had raised his hackles. He needed to possess her to remind them both of what they had.

But Gwen was not so easily convinced. She was, after all, a modern woman accustomed to her independence.

Unlike some women of her acquaintance, she didn't buy the idea that all males secretly longed to turn back the clock and resurrect their once rampant superiority. But she did subscribe to the "give 'em an inch, they'll take a mile" philosophy that suggested it was best to get the ground rules down very firmly right from the start.

"Stop it," she said when she had managed to twist her head to the side, evading the warm, probing invasion of his tongue. "I told you, I don't like this."

"You're lying," he mocked, his free hand caressing her breast, tugging lightly at the nipple, which was already hard with desire.

Scornfully she glared at him. "Don't tell me you're one of those men who thinks a woman means yes when she says no? The mere fact that you can arouse me doesn't mean I want to go to bed with you."

His warm, calloused palm continued to cup her, but tentatively now, as uncertainty swept over him. He would never have thought for a moment that he could be one of those idiots she described, but he had to admit that she had a point. He was pushing her too hard, not taking her feelings into consideration. That was hardly the behavior of a lover.

"I'm sorry," he said with genuine regret as he moved away from her. Wearily he pushed a hand through his hair and shook his head. "The trip must have taken more out of me than I thought. I'm being a bastard."

"No, you aren't," she said, relenting in the face of his obvious remorse. "But we do need to talk. Everything's happened between us so quickly that I have the feeling I'm in over my head. I don't like that."

"All right," he agreed, relieved that she wasn't angrier at him. He really had to get hold of himself. What he'd learned in Cardiff was no excuse for mistreating her. "What do you want to talk about?"

At the moment, nothing. She had to sternly remind herself that there was more at stake here than the momentary satisfaction of rampant hormones. With some difficulty she looked him straight in the eye and said, "You should have told me your real name was James Owens."

It was something of a shot in the dark, since there was still an outside possibility that she could be wrong, or that he would simply deny her suspicions and claim not to know what she was talking about.

Owen did neither. He looked suitably nonplussed for an instant, then threw back his head and laughed.

"I should have known," he said in response to her puzzled stare. "After all these years you *would* be the person to find out. Do you know, not even my publisher suspects the truth."

"Why not? What's the big mystery?"

"It's a long story," he said, his amusement subsiding. "I'll explain it as best I can, but first, tell me, how did you find out?"

"You left a manuscript on your desk. I saw it when I went into the library to find something to read."

Owen shook his head in bewilderment. "I could have sworn I put that thing away before I asked you to stay here."

"I didn't snoop. It was right out in the open."

"I believe you," he said quickly. "Odds are I wanted you to find it. Your knowing does make everything simpler."

"Not from my perspective," she said. "I can't understand why you'd fabricate a false identity."

"It's not completely fabricated. Garrett was my mother's maiden name. But it is true that I've gone to some lengths to obscure who I am."

"Why?" Gwen repeated. "Surely you can't be ashamed of your writing. It's brilliant. And I can't believe that there's anything in your past to justify such duplicity."

He smiled and touched a gentle finger to her lips, tracing their lush curve. "Thank you, your faith in me means a great deal. But the fact is that it's precisely my past that keeps me from living under my real name."

"I don't understand," Gwen said, tasting his skin against her mouth. "You aren't saying that you've done something wrong?"

"No," he assured her quietly. "Nor anything that I'm ashamed of. But I used to live very differently than I do now, and I prefer for that earlier life not to intrude on this one. Unfortunately," he added with a sigh, "that isn't always possible."

"You were a history professor before you became a full-time writer."

"And before that . . . ?" he encouraged her gently.

Her forehead wrinkled. He was leading her somewhere, but she had no idea where. "You traveled around for a while, doing odd jobs, then you must have gone to school. Your academic credentials are certainly complete."

"I didn't start back to school right away. In fact, that wasn't until much later. In between, I was in the army."

"The British Army?"

He smiled. "That's the one Welshmen generally join."

"Well, that must have been interesting. I suppose you got to travel a lot."

"You might say so," he told her, a glint of amusement in his eyes. Her innocence touched him, if only because she was so wise in other ways. "I saw a great deal of the Middle East, as well as Afghanistan, East Germany and Bulgaria."

"But . . . British troops aren't stationed in those places."

"No, but our antiterrorist squads—and yours—sometimes operate there. Behind enemy lines, so to speak."

"Antiterrorist . . . ?"

"I saw history close up," he said tautly. "In the making. It was raw, ugly and insanely bloody. After a few years I decided that I needed some perspective. I was laid up for a while following an injury, so I started taking some courses. One thing led to another, and I realized that I could have an influence in a way that didn't involve constantly killing or the risk of being killed. To be honest about it, I was getting burned out and probably couldn't have lasted much longer, anyway. Fortunately I was smart enough to admit it and make a change."

"So you got out and eventually came to live here. But why the name change?"

"Originally because there were some people still looking for me," he explained. "Wanting to settle old scores. I was hoping to simply avoid them. It didn't work out that way, but by then I was used to being Owen Garrett instead of James Owens, so I stuck with it."

With difficulty Gwen nerved herself to ask, "Are you still in danger?"

"No," he assured her quickly. "Those people aren't . . . around anymore, and I haven't been involved for some time now." The need to be honest with this woman, above all others, forced him to add, "Except in a purely advisory capacity."

Gwen had a feeling she was going to regret it, but she still felt compelled to ask, "What does that mean?"

"Only that I'm occasionally asked to come in and give my opinion on something. See if I can pick out a face in a bit of film, recognize a voice, things along those lines."

"The trip to Cardiff, you said it was business..."

He nodded somberly. "There was a possibility that the bomb that exploded there recently, the one linked to the Prince's visit, was the work of a terrorist faction I'd had some dealings with. They wanted me to go through the file and see if I could spot anything."

"Did you?"

He shook his head. "No, it seems to be a new outfit."

"I'm glad," Gwen murmured, leaning her head against his chest. Instinctively his arms went around her, holding her with gentle strength. "I'm glad," she repeated, more firmly. "It may sound cowardly, but I can't stand the thought of your being swept back into that horrible mess."

Owen stroked her hair tenderly and pressed his lips to her forehead. He could feel her trembling and was struck by the realization that it was out of fear for him. It had been a very long time since anyone had cared so much for him, if ever.

He was used to being on his own, solely responsible for himself and without strong ties to anything other than his own ideals. Sometime in the past few days that had changed.

A part of himself that he had kept tightly clenched and almost furtively hidden had at last unfolded. He loved Gwen, and just the hope that she might return his feelings filled him with fierce joy.

Which meant, unfortunately, that he couldn't bring himself to tell her the rest of what had happened in Cardiff. It might very well amount to nothing, though his instincts were telling him otherwise.

Sooner or later, probably sooner, he would know the truth. In the meantime he chose to let her believe that they were both safe, knowing even as he did so that he might be tragically wrong.

Chapter 13

Two bodies were entwined on the bed, one long, hard, lean, undeniably male; the other smaller, infinitely softer, possessed of fluid curves that molded to the taut expanse of muscle and sinew poised above her. Two pieces of a whole, fitting perfectly together.

The covers were pushed all the way back. One pillow lay beneath Gwen's head, another under her raised hips. Between them her upper body arched, pulled to almost unbearable tightness by the force of her need. Her eyes were closed, her swollen lips parted. She made a soft, whimpering sound deep in her throat and went on making it, helpless to stop.

They had been making love for hours while sunlight faded into dusk and one by one the stars began to shine against the blue-velvet sky. Fierce hunger had been assuaged over and over, only to rise again, more demanding than before. They were in the grip of a power neither could control, but with which they had to come to terms before they could go any further.

"I can't get enough of you," Owen gasped as he raised his head from between her thighs. His eyes glinted dangerously in the fading light. The hours of passion had stripped away the thin veneer of civilization, revealing him as a powerful, proud man, boundlessly generous in his giving, insatiably demanding in his taking.

"Please," Gwen moaned softly, "I can't stand this." She managed, how she didn't know, to half lift herself so that she could reach him, her hands tangling in his thick, damp hair. "It's unbearable." Tears glinted in her eyes. She was actually in pain, a sweet, tearing ache that made her writhe in shameless need.

Owen's big hands rested on her milk-white thighs, his thumbs rubbing the ultrasensitive inner skin, coming close to, but not quite touching, the glistening nest of red-gold curls. "I'll make it better," he promised thickly.

But not just yet. As she had done to him, as he had done to her, again and again, he wanted to draw her up to the highest possible peak, to feel her fly apart into a thousand shards and know that he was responsible for her release.

There was an almost savage element in his taking of her that dismayed him, and might have provoked him to stop if her desire hadn't matched his own. They were equals in this ancient struggle between man and woman; there would be no victor, no vanquished.

That two such overwhelmingly powerful forces could meet without destroying each other was unique in his experience. If the world itself had flown apart beneath them, he would have been only mildly surprised.

With both his tongue and his hands he cherished her body. Lovingly he caressed the hard ridges of her hip bones, relishing the contrast they made to the softness of her belly. He blew gently on her skin, laughing when she shivered with delight.

The hard tip of his tongue circled her navel, delving into it with short, quick thrusts. Her skin was hot and faintly salty, a feast for his own fevered senses.

Desperately Gwen grasped his broad shoulders, her nails digging into the bronzed skin. His lower body had moved over hers, pushing her into the mattress. She needed to rise, to arch and twist, to release at least some of the fierce tension building within her. But she could not, and the frustration of that need pushed her over the edge.

"Damn you," she gasped. "Don't do this to me."

"To both of us," he muttered thickly, turning his attention at last to her breasts. They were high and firm, with dark pink aureoles and erect nipples. They were the most beautiful he had ever seen, and he loved the satiny fullness of them in his hands and mouth.

As he bent his dark head to suckle her, he had the briefest flash of a baby nestled there, and the wave of tenderness that thought provoked all but over-whelmed him. His teeth grazed her lightly, pulling and tugging.

Her back arched as his hands slid beneath her, over her shoulder blades and higher, to hold her still for his sensual torment. Her breath came in harsh gasps.

With a strength she hadn't known she possessed, she managed to wrench her legs from beneath his and twine them around his hips, bringing them together. He was painfully hard, almost scorching to the touch; she was wet and open, demanding the tribute he was so ready to give.

Still he hesitated, driving them both to even higher reaches of need, until at last she wrapped her fingers around him and drew him to her. He braced his hands on the mattress, rising above her, his features pulled taut and his teeth bared, almost in a grimace.

His first thrust brought him fully within her, and for a moment they were both still, eyes locked together, savoring the completeness of their union. Then they began to move in perfect harmony, not gently, as they had before, but with fierce strength.

Despite the nearly intolerable waves of pleasure washing over him, Owen held on to his self-control long enough to glory in the vision of her own release. Only then did his follow as with a harsh cry, he slumped against her.

In the aftermath they were both utterly drained, and they slipped into sleep with their bodies still joined. Sometime in the night a cool breeze blew up. Owen woke groggily and pulled the covers over them. He nestled Gwen in the crook of his shoulder and was asleep again before his eyes were even fully closed.

Gwen woke first, coming reluctantly out of the dim reaches of dreams that had sent tingles of warmth over her body. She felt the roughness of velvet underlaid by steel beneath her cheek and rubbed herself against it.

The corners of her mouth lifted slightly. She was utterly content, replete in every way, or so she thought, until the rumbling of her stomach reminded her of how long it had been since she had eaten. That brought back memories of how the intervening hours had been spent.

She sat up, staring down at Owen with the startled wary look of a forest animal taken by surprise. How had he possibly drawn such raging passion from her, such unabashed sensuality, such blatant demand to both give and receive satisfaction? What previously unsuspected part of herself had he tapped?

The mere study of his features offered no answer except to alert her to the fact that even at his most relaxed he exuded a sense of enormous strength and resoluteness.

Lacking the animation of wakefulness, the harsh lines experience had carved into his face were more apparent. He looked slightly older than his thirty-five years, with no hint of softness or yielding.

Staring at him, she remembered what he had told her about his background and wondered why she hadn't guessed before, not at the details but at the

overall truth: he was a man who had faced the harsh-
est side of life without having his essential ideals in the
least diminished.

There was nothing cynical about the firm cast of his
mouth, no hint of irresolution in the shadowed contours of his lean cheeks and jaw. He confronted life in
all its unpredictable, exultant, juicy reality—and
compelled her to do the same.

Which, she had to admit, she greatly enjoyed.

With an utterly feminine smile she slipped from the
bed and padded across the room to the closet. She
supposed a shower was in order, but she was in no
hurry to wash the smell and feel of him from her skin
and replace it with some prettified synthetic scent. She
could revel in it a while longer without feeling in the
least abashed.

In the same way she reveled in the touch of the blue
silk robe against her sensitized flesh. She didn't bother
to fasten it, but instead walked over to the dresser,
where she had left her hairbrush.

Standing at the window, looking out pensively at the
early morning countryside, she brushed the tangles
from her gleaming hair with sure, steady strokes.

Until the prickling at the back of her neck told her
that she was being watched. Owen lay with his arms
folded under his head, his eyes hooded, with the
expression of a sated cat. When she turned and the
open robe gave him a long, unhindered look at her
nudity, he smiled and stretched languidly.

"Come over here," he said, satiation fading quickly.

She touched the tip of her tongue between her white teeth and shook her head. "I don't think so."

"Why not?"

"Because I'm hungry—for food."

"You said that yesterday, and look what it led to."

"Can you live on air?" she teased, fighting the temptation to go to him. He'd had the initiative long enough; next time it would be hers.

"I can live on you," he said, and the expression in his eyes made it clear that he was ready and more than willing to devour her yet again.

"You're a romantic," she said as though she had just discovered it, when in fact the suspicion had been growing in her for some time.

"Guilty, though I never knew it before."

"You thought raising falcons and renovating an old monastery was practical, everyday stuff?"

Rather than answer her directly, he said, "Sweetheart, if you're going to stand there in that delightful state of dishabille, this not a good time to discuss anything related to the previous purpose of this building. Not unless you want to have the good monks revolving in their graves."

Gwen glanced down at herself, saw what he had been admiring and managed a delightfully unconcerned shrug even as she belted her robe. "It is a bit chilly."

"Come back to bed and I'll warm you."

"Come down to the kitchen and I'll feed you," she countered.

"You're a hard woman."

"Speaking of hard..."

"Now, now," he said as he swung his long legs over the edge of the bed and stood up. He was glorious in his nakedness, tall and lean, his skin burnished by the early morning sunlight, his masculinity blatant.

Conscious of her admiring appraisal, he hid a smile as he took his time finding a robe and putting it on. "Get a move on, woman," he said with mock sternness. "I've decided I need to be fed, after all."

"If this were Boston," she muttered as they headed for the kitchen, "we could call out for pizza, and while we waited for it to get here we could—"

"A very civilized custom," Owen acknowledged, "having food delivered. But tell me, what else do you miss about Boston?"

Gwen opened the refrigerator, took out the lamb she had prepared during his absence and began slicing it before she answered. "It's hard to say." Very, since she was racking her brains to think of a single thing. That certainly took her aback. Surely there should be something she missed. "I've only been away a short time," she hedged finally.

"No yearnings for familiar scenes, familiar people? You don't miss your home, or anyone in particular?"

"I...miss walking on the Commons, browsing through the bookstores, watching the skiffs on the

Charles River.'' She was grasping at straws. Those were no more than pleasant diversions.

''You can walk all you want here, and Wales happens to have a long tradition of fine bookstores. If it's rowing you want, I'll be happy to oblige, though I warn you that the waters around here are a good deal more exciting than any tame river.''

Touched by his determination to convince her that she could have everything she wanted right where she was, she said lightly, ''Why don't we just admit that Wales is perfect and leave it at that?''

''No,'' he said as he took the plates from her and set the table, ''it's not. We've got our share of problems, perhaps even a bit more.''

''That's good.'' At his surprised look, she explained, ''To live somewhere with no problems would be like moving into a completely artificial environment, a fantasy island sort of place. I couldn't stand that.''

''But you could stand Wales, warts and all?'' He tried to make the question sound casual, but couldn't entirely succeed, not when so much was at stake.

Gwen sat down at the table and busied herself putting a sandwich together, meanwhile considering her words with care. She owed it to both of them to answer as honestly and completely as she could.

''I'm falling in love with Wales,'' she told him candidly, not adding, though she could have, *and with you.* ''I feel very much at home here, but,'' she went on quickly when he would have spoken, ''that doesn't mean I can give up my life in the States and move here. For one thing, there's the question of what I would do.''

"Do?"

"For a living. I enjoy my job a great deal, and, aside from the fact that I need the income, I'm not sure I could find anything comparable here.''

"It's true the demand for specialists in medieval art probably isn't all that great," he admitted reluctantly.

"And what demand there is must be more than satisfied by the people who are already here.''

"Isn't there anything else you'd be interested in doing?''

Gwen hesitated. She was reluctant to admit her dream, even to him, if only because she didn't want to sound presumptuous. At length she said, "Actually, I've always wanted to write.''

His face, somber a moment before, lit up. Here was something he could help her with. "About medieval art? That's great. I can put you in touch with all the right people. In fact, we could work together.''

"Hold on a minute. What I have in mind is fiction.''

"Fiction?'' He sounded as if he had no idea what that was, despite the wide selection of novels in his office.

"I always have," she explained patiently. "Since I was a little girl. And I know what you're going to say," she added before he could interrupt. "It's a very precarious way to try to make a living. But sometimes I think if I never give it a try, I'll never be satisfied with myself."

"Then by all means try. Do you have an idea for a book?"

"Yes," she admitted, and that alone was considerably more than she had told anyone else. "It's a historical novel set in the Middle Ages. It makes use of my background in medieval art, but it also has to do with a lot of other things."

"Such as?"

"It's, uh, something of a romance."

His smile widened. "Steamy, is it?"

"I suppose you might say so." In fact, the half-dozen chapters she had written so far, working evenings and weekends, had surprised her with their sensuality. She hadn't known where such thoughts were coming from, until she met Owen.

"It sounds to me," he said, "as though it might turn out to be very commercial."

"That's not why I want to write it. I just love the story."

"Still, you wouldn't hate making money from it. I didn't, and heaven knows it was the last thing I expected to happen."

"No," Gwen admitted, "I wouldn't hate it. That way I could write full-time."

"All the time?" he asked. "Or would you perhaps be willing to take on a few other activities, as well?"

The look he gave her made it clear what he had in mind. She laughed and shook her head reprovingly. "Don't you ever think of anything else?"

He pretended to be wounded, but the devilment dancing in his eyes put the lie to it. "Of course. Eating, for instance, which, if you notice, we've finished doing."

So they had. Which left all sorts of possibilities.

"Shouldn't we feed the animals?" Gwen asked.

"I put out extra for them yesterday. They'll be fine for a while."

"I really need to go back to Myrddin's Rock, if only to see if the power's been fixed."

The mention of the castle broke the teasingly sensual mood, at least for Owen. It reminded him of the danger she had been in, and of the suspicions that were beginning to form in his mind.

He had come back from Cardiff determined to put his concerns to rest, one way or the other, and already he had spent a day in unrelated pursuits, however enjoyable. He could hardly think of the time as wasted, but it was a measure of how far he had come from the relentlessly directed man he had once been that he had allowed himself to be led astray.

She distracted him to an extraordinary degree; in her arms he forgot even the most fundamental principles by which he had lived so much of his life, namely to take nothing for granted and to trust no one.

He wanted to lock out all the rest of the world and pretend that nothing could ever hurt them, a singularly unrealistic fantasy he was determined to put an end to.

"Now that I think of it," he said, "there are several things I need to do. Why don't you take it easy for a while, and when I get back we'll go over to Myrddin's Rock together?"

Gwen looked at him in surprise. His abrupt shift in mood dismayed her. She had fully expected him to coax her back into the bedroom and had been prepared to put up only the most token reluctance. Now, suddenly, without explanation, he apparently had more pressing concerns.

It was neither flattering nor reassuring. "Fine," she said stiffly, turning her back on him.

Owen cursed under his breath. He had hurt her without meaning to, and his clumsiness appalled him. For all his experience he was a novice when it came to dealing with the feelings of a woman he cared for deeply.

He put a hand on her shoulder. "What I meant was..."

She shook his hand off. "It doesn't matter. I've got to take a shower."

They were going to have to work on better communication, he decided as he watched her walk away. Getting along fantastically in bed was great, but he wanted much more. He was ready for it and, if he knew anything at all, so was she.

For the moment he would let her go, but it was past time for the two of them to come to a reckoning, and he didn't intend to delay it an instant longer than he had to. The sooner he settled the issues that had been raised in Cardiff, the sooner he could get on with the rest of his life.

Chapter 14

After she had showered and dressed Gwen felt a little better. It wasn't like her to be so ultrasensitive, but she had the good sense to accept it as part of the price of being in love. It stood to reason that even the smallest nuances of Owen's behavior would affect her deeply. She would simply have to get used to that if they were to make a life together.

That was not the same thing as saying that she had to accept whatever he chose to dish out, however. The broad streak of independence that was like a steel ribbon winding through her nature had not been changed. She could share herself without losing what was intrinsic to her being.

It was all very well for him to expect her to sit around waiting for his return, but that didn't happen to suit her. Better he should learn right away not to take her compliance for granted.

Owen had barely left the house, Lancelot at his heels, than Gwen did the same. She drove into the village, intending to pick up a few things at Mrs. Gascoigne's, not so much because she needed them as because she felt like socializing.

The elderly lady was busy with another customer when Gwen arrived, a plump, pigeon-chested matron who eyed her warily before venturing a small smile. Gwen returned it, but did not attempt to strike up a conversation. She had the sense that she was no longer considered quite so much a stranger. If she stayed, she might eventually be accepted into the life of the village, provided that she didn't try to push her way in too quickly.

"You're looking very well, dear," Mrs. Gascoigne said when they were alone in the sawdust-scented store. "Our little corner of the world seems to agree with you."

The wry glance that accompanied these seemingly innocuous words disquieted Gwen. It hadn't occurred to her that her relationship with Owen might become known so quickly.

Telling herself not to jump to unwarranted conclusions, she said, "It's quite a change from Boston. Much less hectic."

"I'm sure that's true. Give me the quiet life anytime, not that I've ever known anything else, mind you. But this suits me well enough. Here a person has time to take note of events and consider them. Have you ever read Agatha Christie, dear?''

"Yes, as a matter of fact, I have," Gwen said.

"Then you're familiar with Miss Marple. Such a fascinating character; I feel as though we've been neighbors these many years. She always says that living in a little village affords one all the same experiences as a big city would, because all the same types of people are gathered there. It's possible to learn an enormous amount about human nature from watching it up close."

"Is that what you are, Mrs. Gascoigne?" Gwen asked with a smile. "A student of human nature?"

"Who among us isn't, dear? We're always striving to understand ourselves and others. Sometimes I think that's the sole purpose of life. But enough of such serious talk. What can I get for you?"

Gwen gave her a short list and waited while the older woman bustled about assembling the items. She would have helped, but this was Mrs. Gascoigne's domain, and the old woman subscribed to the belief that customers were to be waited on, not to help themselves to whatever they happened to want.

She was totaling up the prices, when Gwen said, "Do you really think that all sorts of people come together in a small village like this?"

Her black eyes glittered brightly as Mrs. Gascoigne nodded. "Oh, yes, indeed. Outsiders always think that country people are simple sorts, uncomplicated and straightforward. But nothing could be further from the truth. We have the full spectrum of human emotions—good and bad—right here."

"It's hard to believe," Gwen admitted. "In Boston we're used to hearing about all sorts of things. I stopped turning on the radio in the morning because I couldn't take hearing about all the terrible crimes that had happened during the night. The repeated violence and cruelty made me want to creep back under the covers and hide."

"Violence is everywhere," Mrs. Gascoigne said quietly. "You can try to escape from it, but it follows wherever you go."

"You really believe that?" Gwen asked.

"Oh, yes. Why, only a few years ago we had a string of murders not far from here. Three young girls were strangled. The killer turned out to be a very nice boy who lived with his mother and did odd jobs for the neighbors. No one wanted to believe it at first, but the evidence was clear. He'd killed them, all right. What's more, he wasn't even sorry for it."

"He couldn't possibly have claimed what he did was justified," Gwen said, appalled at the thought of young lives so carelessly snuffed out, especially in a place where they should have been safe.

"Yes, he did," Mrs. Gascoigne said. "They'd snubbed him, you see. Wouldn't go to the teen dances with him. He thought that made what he did all right. People," she added, looking at Gwen directly, "can come up with excuses for the worst sort of behavior. In fact, the more mayhem they commit, the more likely they are to claim they had a perfect right to do so.''

Gwen thought of the terrorists Owen had battled and the rationales they put forward for the most horrendous brutality. She nodded slowly. ''Yes, you're right, but surely what happened here, terrible as it was, was an isolated incident.''

''I'd certainly like to think so,'' Mrs. Gascoigne agreed. ''But I haven't lived as long as I have without learning the pitfalls of wishful thinking. No, I never presume that the worst isn't possible.''

''I wouldn't have thought you had that kind of outlook. You always seem so cheerful.''

''It hardly pays to go around long faced and down at the mouth. But I keep my eyes open, and I think about what I see. What I hear, too.''

Gwen was silent for a moment. She knew that she could choose to end the conversation right there and walk away, or she could pursue it and possibly discover what was troubling Mrs. Gascoigne. That she was troubled was clear. She had deliberately raised the subject of dire deeds committed in bucolic places and seemed to be going out of her way to warn Gwen.

The temptation not to listen was almost irresistible, but it had never been her way to hide her head in the sand. Resolutely she said gently, ''If something is worrying you, I wish you'd just come straight out and tell me about it. Perhaps I could help.''

Mrs. Gascoigne sighed. She sat down on her stool behind the counter and looked at her gnarled hands, folded in the lap of her black serge skirt. After a moment her mouth trembled. "I'm sorry, dear. You're going to think I'm a foolish old woman bidding after attention."

"No, I'm not. You're the farthest thing from foolish. Besides, you were Winny's friend, and I hope you'll be mine, too. I wouldn't like to think that you couldn't speak frankly to me."

"You're a good girl. Winny was right to trust you."

"I hope so," Gwen said softly. "But now, please tell me what the trouble is."

"Nothing I can put my finger on," Mrs. Gascoigne said. "But I've noticed a series of small things that don't seem to add up right." She picked up the stubby pencil she habitually used and stared at it absently. "Daniel was in here this morning with another man, a rough-looking sort. I overheard him—Daniel, that is—saying that he'd told you about the offer on Myrddin's Rock and he thought you'd have the sense to take it."

"That's what has you concerned, that I'm going to sell the house?"

"I certainly shouldn't like you to," Mrs. Gascoigne acknowledged. "But it was more than that. Daniel seemed so nervous. He couldn't bring himself to look at the man directly, and he was too polite to him, as though something frightened him. I've never seen him behave like that before. Frankly, the way he was raised and what he's made of himself, he's not inclined to be deferential to anyone."

"He does have to work for a living," Gwen reminded her. "And sometimes he must have to be especially polite to clients."

"I could see that if the other man had seemed a very smooth, successful type. But he was carelessly dressed, hadn't shaved...why, he looked more like a thug than anyone Daniel would represent."

That did seem curious. So far as Gwen knew, Daniel had a perfectly respectable business that dealt with what in the States would be called family law, primarily wills, estates, properties and so on. He was certainly not a criminal attorney who would be required to mix with the sort of person Mrs. Gascoigne seemed to be describing.

More puzzling still was what that sort of person could possibly have to do with the offer for Myrddin's Rock. "It's true that a very generous offer has been made," Gwen said, "but I haven't decided to accept it. One of the reasons is that Daniel won't reveal the identity of the would-be buyer."

"That is odd. Did he give a reason why?"

"No, but it doesn't really matter, because I don't think I'm going to accept." Putting into words what she had previously only been thinking made her feel at once more certain and relieved.

The matter of her legacy had been weighing more heavily on her than she realized. Complicated as everything was by her relationship with Owen, she had been reluctant to commit herself to the house before she could be sure of the man. Now she was no longer waiting for that certainty, but instead taking the initiative and deciding her own future.

"I'm not going to sell Myrddin's Rock," she said firmly. "It will stay in my family for as long as I have anything to say about it."

"That's wonderful news," Mrs. Gascoigne said with a broad smile. "Winny would be very happy. But . . ." the smile faded, "Daniel may be upset."

"I can't help that. He'll simply have to accept my decision." But she could at least do him the courtesy of telling him promptly and in person. "Is he usually in his office at this hour?"

Mrs. Gascoigne nodded. "Most likely. But, dear, perhaps, just to avoid any unpleasantness, you should ask Owen to drop by with you."

Reminding herself that the elderly lady was of a generation where women commonly shied away from confrontations and sought the protection of men, Gwen said gently, "I think I can take care of it myself."

"Still, Owen might prefer that you let him—"

"Whatever Owen prefers," Gwen interrupted, "I have to handle my own affairs. Besides," she added for good measure, "it would hardly be fair to impose on him for help when we've only known each other such a short time."

She could have sworn that Mrs. Gascoigne chuckled, though the sound was quickly suppressed. "Whatever you say, dear, though in my day it wasn't the length of the acquaintance that mattered so much as, shall we say, the intensity.''

Gwen shook her head wryly. ''Is there anything you don't know about?''

''A great deal,'' Mrs. Gascoigne allowed modestly. ''But something for you to remember about living in the country, especially this country. It puts a person in tune with nature. We're all part of something much bigger than ourselves, and all we've been able to do so far is sniff around the edges of it.''

Her wise, bright eyes looked out the window at distant horizons. ''This place . . .'' she said slowly. ''For thousands of years, from the earliest legends, there have been special powers here. Magic, if you like. No one nowadays wants to believe in that. We'd rather believe in machines. They demand so much less of us, but they also give less.''

Gwen heard her out in silence. She thought of her own life in Boston, where she was surrounded by the products of high technology to such an extent that she took them for granted. Her work provided some balance, but hardly enough to offset the continual barrage of what she had to admit were often dehumanizing influences.

Other people besides herself were beginning to realize that. Witness the demonstrations against nuclear weapons and power plants, the efforts to stop acid rain, and so on.

Whatever the merits of individual cases, they seemed to represent a growing understanding that something was badly out of kilter. Humanity had cut itself off from something essential to its survival, something the wise old woman claimed still dwelt in the green hills of Wales.

"Keep talking like this," Gwen said softly, "and you'll have me believing in dragons."

Mrs. Gascoigne smiled. "I think you already do, dear."

Be that as it may, once she stood outside, blinking in the sunlight, the entire conversation in the shop had an air of unreality about it, almost as though it had been a dream. She had solid, practical problems to deal with, starting with Daniel. No dragon would be able to help her there.

Not that she needed help. She would simply explain to him that she had changed her mind about selling. And while she was at it, she would ask who exactly he had found to buy the property, what sort of scruffy creep he had thought would be a fitting master of Myrddin's Rock.

By the time she climbed the stairs to Daniel's office she was feeling in fine fettle. She would polish him off as an appetizer before heading back to the monastery and letting Owen know what she thought of his high-handedness. They'd get a thing or two settled between them and then...

"And I'm telling you," an angry voice said from behind the office door, "we can wait no longer. We want her out *now*."

"Of course, of course," Daniel murmured. "I understand completely, but—"

"Do I have to remind you, Pierce, that this was your idea? You convinced us that if we put up enough money she'd take it. Now what the hell's gone wrong?"

"Nothing, nothing at all. She simply needs time to think it over. Is that so hard to understand? After all, the property has been in her family for centuries. She feels a certain . . . responsibility."

"If she's holding out for more, she won't get it. We've got a budget, you know."

"For God's sake, Henry," Daniel protested. "I'm perfectly aware that our funds aren't unlimited. Generous as our . . . backers are, they do have limits."

"There are . . . other methods."

"No! That is, there's no reason. The last thing we want to do is call attention to ourselves."

There was a pause before the other man said sneeringly, "You wouldn't be personally involved here, would you? I've heard she's a damn good-looking woman."

"Don't be ridiculous. I'm simply being reasonable. Remember where carelessness and impulsiveness got us just a few days ago."

"That was an accident."

"It could still have serious repercussions, if they've found anything to connect us—"

"Stop worrying about it," the other man ordered. "Just take care of the woman, or by God, the rest of us will."

Gwen didn't wait to hear anything more. She turned around, ran down the steps and kept going until she reached her car. Not until she was safe inside it did she pause to catch her breath and wonder at what she had heard.

No matter how she considered it, she couldn't make it add up to anything except trouble. Daniel was involved with people who didn't seem overly scrupulous about how they achieved their objectives. Perhaps some perfectly legitimate enterprises were conducted that way, but she tended to doubt it. There had been a distinct flavor of illegality about what she had overheard. And the reference to recent carelessness and what it might lead to...

She had to talk to Owen, if only so he could tell her that her imagination was running wild and that there was really nothing to be concerned about.

Except that when she got back to the monastery there was still no sign of him. Irritated as much by her own growing worry as by his absence, she stood uncertainly for a moment in the center of the entry hall before abruptly deciding that it was better to do something than nothing.

To sit and wait for him would only exacerbate her concern, when she could at least be getting something useful done by sticking to her original intention of checking on Myrddin's Rock.

Even after so short an absence she was glad to see the ancient round tower appear at the end of the road. She parked her car and hurried inside, wasting no time before flicking the light switch to confirm that the power had been restored.

Next on her agenda was a look at the storeroom steps that had caused her accident. She approached them with trepidation, but by going carefully managed to avoid the broken step and reach the bottom safely.

Examining the stairs from below, she noted that the wood was newer and more solid than she had thought. She had presumed it had simply rotted through due to dampness and age, but now she had to wonder what had caused the collapse.

There was no sign of anything else amiss in the storeroom. Neat rows of shelves held cans, and there were bins of dry goods. Off to one side were several trunks that Gwen promised herself she would look into before much longer. If they contained anything useful or interesting they should be moved upstairs to protect them from the humidity.

It was very damp in the storeroom, enough so that the whitewashed walls were stained in patches by a faintly phosphorescent green growth. Perhaps that was the result of an underground stream, or perhaps the sea had carved a hidden channel that came up under the house.

Gwen touched a hand lightly to the nearest wall. It was cool and slightly slick, definitely indicating the presence of water nearby. If it was the sea, that might explain the legends of caves beneath the house. The action of the waves and the tide would have carved them out long ago, and the rumbling of the water passing between stone walls might explain the tremors she had felt.

Excited as she was by the prospect of solving the mystery of that strange phenomenon, she was nonetheless unwilling to linger overly long in the storeroom. Its dankness and the memory of her recent accident discouraged her. It was with relief that she climbed carefully back up the stairs, put away the items she had picked up in the village and considered what to do next.

Logically, she should return to Owen's house. There was plenty to occupy her there in his absence: books to read, animals to play with, treasures to enjoy. She'd been meaning to take a closer look at the tapestries and at the part of the building still awaiting restoration.

But she was loath to be found there waiting for him like an obedient little female. Instead she decided on a walk down to the beach, where she hoped the sea breezes would clear her head and allow her to come to some conclusions about herself, Myrddin's Rock and what lay ahead.

Chapter 15

Owen had also headed for the beach, though for a very different purpose than Gwen. He approached it circuitously, using the tall grass at the top of the cliffs to conceal himself.

For a long time he lay in wait, watching the entrance of the cave. When he was finally convinced that nothing stirred there, he made his way down through the clumps of gorse and heather and cautiously entered the narrow recess.

He had brought a powerful flashlight with which he illuminated the interior, disturbing several small things that scurried and fluttered away. When he reached the spot he was looking for, he bent over and examined the damp sand beneath his feet carefully.

Only the most discerning eye could have made out the treads of rubber soled shoes, their markings all but erased by the moisture in the cave. He estimated that, faint as they were, they had been made no more than twelve hours before. The thought of the cave having been used so recently made him frown.

From his pocket he removed the object he had picked up on his earlier visit and studied it. It resembled the standard type of cap for plastique explosives. But in Cardiff he had learned that it was a new, improved version, only beginning to be seen, principally in armaments shipped through the Middle East.

Which hardly explained what it had been doing in a quiet, seaside cave in Wales.

Or, for that matter, in a house in Cardiff that had been destroyed by a premature explosion that had taken the lives of several terrorists while leaving few clues to their identity or aim.

The men in Cardiff—assembled from several top antiterrorist groups and all well-known to him—were convinced something big was in the works. There had been hints from any number of sources: radio transmissions, intercepted cables, tapped telephone calls, the reports of informers and the movements of known terrorists as they made their way around the world, leaving a trail of hatred and death.

That the Prince of Wales might be the intended target, and Wales the intended location, was a possibility because of recent steps England had taken in concert with her allies to punish terrorists. It was al-

ways possible to make mistakes about such things—
false alarms had been given in the past—but Owen had
a niggling feeling that this time the fears were on target.

Which left very little time to find and stop the terrorists. Grimly aware that he might be following a cold
trail, or even a false one, Owen nonetheless pushed on.
With the help of the flashlight he reached much farther into the cave than he had before. It angled downward, the way becoming ever steeper. The air grew
cold and damp, but remained fresh enough to breathe,
telling him that there was ample circulation from the
surface.

The ground beneath his feet gradually changed from
sandy soil to hard rock. Limestone stalactites hung
from the ceiling; he often had to duck to avoid them.
A small channel of water ran off to one side. When he
bent to taste it he discovered to his surprise that it was
fresh, not salt.

The downward slant of the cave was leading him in
the direction of Myrddin's Rock. He suspected that he
had stumbled across an underground stream that
might once have served the castle, particularly during
times of siege.

That meant that the cave ran very deeply into the
cliff, at least as far as Gwen's house, and that some
part of the ancient legend was therefore true.

He was thinking that over when he rounded a corner and stopped abruptly. Ahead lay a large, shadowed mass he could not immediately identify. Not

until he pointed the flashlight beam directly at it did he recognize the outline of several large wooden crates covered with a tarpaulin.

Grimly he bent to examine his find. The letters stenciled on the crates were in the Cyrillic alphabet. Owen's Russian had gotten little use in recent years, but he remembered enough to make out the warning Danger: Explosives and the name of the munitions factory where they had been made.

The route the armaments had taken from their point of origin, and whether or not their movements had been officially sanctioned or were the result of an arms theft, were unknown to him. But in the final analysis it didn't matter. What counted was that there were enough explosives hidden in the cave to destroy several square city blocks. In Cardiff, for instance.

An angry curse broke from him. It was bad enough that such weapons of death and destruction should be hidden anywhere in Wales. That they should turn up virtually on his own doorstep aroused his territorial instincts and made him all the more determined that whoever was responsible for them being there should bear the full brunt of justice.

The peace and tranquillity he had sought for so long, and had at last found, would not be destroyed. Not even if he had to give his life in exchange.

He squatted on his heels to examine the crates more carefully, seeing as he did so that they had not yet been opened. That much at least was in his favor. He suspected that he had found the terrorists' entire cache intact, before any part of it could be moved.

He was considering what to do—whether to leave the crates where they were and go for assistance, or stay and try to learn the identity of the terrorists—when the decision was taken out of his hands. Voices reached him from near the entrance to the cave, drifting ever closer down the deep well of the passageway.

Swiftly he clicked off the flashlight and moved back into the darkness.

Gwen noticed the small van parked near the beach road but thought little of it. Fishermen must use the beach occasionally, or perhaps picnickers had wandered by. Mildly disappointed to have her solitude interrupted, she continued on down the sandy path to the water's edge, determined to enjoy herself.

The sky was clear, and a fresh wind blew out of the west, redolent of the fertile hills of nearby Ireland. She wandered along, kicking absently at stray shells and watching small birds darting back and forth at the tide line.

Gradually a sense of peacefulness stole over her, the source only slowly becoming clear. There on the beach, remembering the hours she had spent with Owen, she felt very much at home. Not even so much with the place itself as with the thought of the man. Hesitantly, almost afraid to believe, she was beginning to suspect that anywhere he happened to be was where she would belong.

The thought confirmed her growing conviction of how much she loved him, enough certainly to work very hard for a future together no matter what adjustments and concessions might be necessary.

He had asked her if she would miss Boston, and in the golden aftermath of lovemaking she had minimized her feelings. But now she realized that if she stayed she would be giving up a great deal from her former life. The key was that she felt the sacrifice would be worthwhile.

And Owen would be making sacrifices, too. His way of life would change as much as hers. He would no longer be the solitary, self-sufficient man she sensed he had always been. He would have to open his heart as well as his life to her. Indeed, she suspected that he already had.

The thought made her all the more eager to find him. The conversation she had overheard outside Daniel's office was still on her mind, but it had assumed far less importance in the face of her concentration on Owen. She still intended to mention it to him, but they had so many other things to talk about that mattered so much more.

She was about to turn around, to head back up the pathway and return to the monastery, when a flicker of movement farther up the cliffside drew her attention. For a moment she thought she had imagined it, until she looked more closely and saw it again, as though someone were moving near the entrance to the cave.

The possibility that it might be Owen made her decide to take a look.

She heard the voices almost as soon as she entered the cave. Two men somewhere ahead of her, talking angrily.

"It's ridiculous to come here in broad daylight. We're simply asking for trouble."

Daniel? Even allowing for the distortion caused by the cave walls, she had no difficulty recognizing his voice. Nor was she really surprised that he would know about the cave, since he had told her himself that he had once roamed all over the area as a boy.

"I had to verify that everything was in order," the other man said, the same one she had overheard in his office. He spoke calmly enough, but with an undertone of annoyance that suggested his nerves were on edge. "We're going to move them out tonight."

"Already?" Daniel asked. "Is that wise?"

"Are you questioning orders?"

"No, of course not. It just seems to me that it would be better to leave them here until they're needed, rather than take the chance of storing them where they might be discovered."

"They could be found here," the other man pointed out. "You're not the only one who knows about this cave, and with that girl still on the scene . . ."

"She's not going to find anything," Daniel insisted.

"No? The cave runs up under the house, and you've told me yourself that it figures in legends about the place. All she has to do is get curious and—"

"That's why we're getting her out."

"You mean we're trying to. Your extravagant solution isn't working."

"Don't start in on that again," Daniel said. "If we play our cards right we can use the cave for a long time to come. But if we start putting too much pressure on Gwen to sell, she's bound to get suspicious and dig her heels in. Why risk wrecking such a perfect setup just to get her out a little faster?"

"It is ideal," the other man admitted. "Access by both road and water, only a small population to deal with, and plenty of escape routes should the need arise. She's the only fly in the ointment, so one way or another she has to go."

"Fine, fine," Daniel said nervously. "Now that you've seen what you wanted to, let's head back. I never liked this place, and I don't intend to hang around any longer than I have to."

The other man laughed derisively. "What's the matter? Those old legends getting to you, too?"

Daniel didn't bother to answer. He turned away and marched swiftly toward the cave entrance, only to stumble over a protruding stone. As he straightened, rubbing his shin and muttering to himself, he saw the shape of a woman silhouetted against the bright sunlight streaming in from outside.

"What . . . ?"

"Daniel," Gwen murmured, caught off guard and frozen in place. She knew that what she had overheard was more damning than the conversation in his office, and because of that she should flee. But nothing in her experience had taught her to deal with such a situation. She was caught by her own surprise, pinned as neatly as a butterfly to a collector's board.

But only for an instant. The sight of the other man's dark, twisted face looming behind Daniel's restored her sense of self-preservation. She whirled around and raced back toward the cave entrance.

She had almost made it, her hand reaching toward the sunlight, when a hard tackle brought her down, driving the air from her lungs and sending her whirling into unconsciousness.

She came to propped up against a wall of the cave. Daniel was sitting beside her on a wooden crate, his face pale and grim. His shoulders were stooped; he looked as though he were carrying the weight of the world. When he felt her eyes on him, he sighed deeply.

"I wish you hadn't come here, Gwen."

"Yes," she breathed softly, "I'm having the same regrets." His somberness and his unwillingness to meet her gaze filled her with dread. She didn't want to believe that she was in serious trouble, but the reality was becoming harder and harder to deny.

"You should have taken the offer and gotten out," Daniel went on. "Do you have any idea how hard it was for me to convince them to spend that kind of money? I had to use all my powers of persuasion to protect you."

"Is that what you were doing?"

"It was the only thing I could think of. If you found out what was going on..." He turned away from her, and she saw that his mouth and chin were trembling. "But you have found out, haven't you? And now..."

"Daniel, however bad this is, there's no point in making it worse. Let me go."

He looked at her in surprise. "I can't do that. Henry would never allow it."

"Where is...?"

"He's gone to check the beach and make sure no one else is around. He had some idea Owen might have been with you."

"What does he know about Owen?" she asked nervously.

Daniel shrugged and reached into the pocket of his jacket for a cigarette. He lit it with a shaking hand. The smell of acrid smoke made Gwen's stomach pitch.

"While you were unconscious Henry wanted to know who you were close to around here, who you might have told where you were going. I told him about Owen."

He said it with such malicious satisfaction that she was prompted to lash back at him. "You wasted your time. We're only friends."

"Don't lie to me," he snarled suddenly. "I saw the two of you on the beach. He's been hot after you from the start, and he's gotten what he wanted, hasn't he?"

Furiously she said, "That's none of your business."

His hand lashed out, grasping her chin and twisting painfully. "Stupid bitch! After what I tried to do for you."

"I'm not the stupid one," Gwen hissed from between clenched teeth. He was hurting her badly, but she would be damned if she would let him see that. "It's you, playing at being what—a revolutionary?—pretending to care about your country when all you really care about are your own hatreds and resentments. You're like all the rest of them, violent, callous, as low as a human being can be. But you won't succeed. You'll be st—"

"Shut up!" he demanded, his other hand twisting in her hair and wrenching her head back. He had slid off the packing crate and was kneeling in front of her, his face mere inches from hers. She could see the light of maddened rage in his eyes and hear the harsh rasp of his breathing as he bent even closer.

"You don't know what you're talking about. You've had everything all your life. Everything's been easy for you, but now you're going to have to pay."

She wanted to tell him what nonsense that was, that she had worked hard all her life and earned everything she had. But the words stuck in her throat as she realized how singularly ineffective they would be.

Daniel was a fanatic who saw the world in his own distorted terms. He was beyond being reached by any appeal to reason. But he was not beyond emotion, as he had showed when he tried, however ineffectively, to protect her.

"You should have been nicer to me," he said plaintively, "instead of to Owen. He can't help you, but I can."

Gwen understood perfectly well what he was telling her, but the mere idea of what his help would cost her made her recoil. Even if her feelings for Owen had not been a consideration, she couldn't bear the touch of such a man for any reason.

He saw that, and his expression turned ugly again. "You think you're too good for me, don't you? Well, you're wrong. You're nothing but a little whore, going with Owen, letting him touch you. Did you like the things he did?" he demanded, his hand sliding down to painfully grasp her arm. "I'll bet you did. I'll bet you—"

Whatever else Daniel had intended to say, the words never came. As Gwen watched, caught between horror and disbelief, his eyes opened wide, he gasped once for breath that would not come, then crumpled silently at her feet.

Pale and shaking, she looked up to see Owen standing remorselessly above her. "W-what...did you...?"

"He isn't dead," he said matter-of-factly. "Though he would have been if I'd pressed a bit harder." With the tip of his boot he turned Daniel over and looked at him dispassionately. "I considered it, but it would be useful to have him alive to question later."

Gwen shivered. She didn't recognize this man, so hard and cold. But she could sense the implacable rage in him, made all the more dangerous by the strict restraint he was so clearly exercising.

When he held out a hand she hesitated a moment. He didn't wait for her, but grasped her firmly and pulled her to her feet. "The other one could be back anytime. We have to move."

"Henry..." she gasped. "That's his name. I heard it at Daniel's office."

He cast her a quick look that told her nothing. "You'll have to tell me what else you heard."

"Not much, but enough to figure out something was wrong. They're the terrorists, aren't they?"

He nodded. "Pierce is strictly local, but Henry is a different story. His last name's Wilshire, and he's been implicated in bombings from Tokyo to London."

"They wanted the house," she said breathlessly as she hurried to keep up with him, "because it connects somehow to the cave." They were moving toward the entrance, but as they reached it, Owen stopped abruptly and pushed her back against the wall.

"Wait here," he ordered.

"Where are you...?"

He didn't answer her, but moved swiftly and silently into the sunlight, using the rocky sides of the entrance to conceal himself. She waited in the darkness, heart pounding, mouth dry. Never had she felt so alone, so cut off from everything safe and secure.

She was completely out of her element, but Owen was in his.

Gone was the sensitive discoverer of the past, the cherisher of tradition, the brilliant historian. Gone even was the lover who had roused her to such peaks of ecstasy with such exquisite tenderness. There was only a relentless, threatening stranger who seemed perfectly at home in a world of almost incomprehensible violence.

He returned while she was still pondering this, looked at her pale, drawn face and said shortly, "He's coming back. Get down behind those rocks and stay there until I tell you it's safe to come out."

"What are you going to do?" she demanded, unable to simply obey him.

A look of impatience flitted over his stark features, as though he were annoyed at having to spell it out for her. "I'm going to stop him."

"The way you stopped Daniel?"

He shrugged, as though it really weren't all that important. "If I can."

"Otherwise..."

"Otherwise I'm going to kill him before he gets a chance to kill us or anyone else. Is that enough for you to know? Will you get down behind the rocks now?"

Numbly Gwen nodded. She felt foolish, on top of being frightened. It was a bad combination. Tears stung her eyes, and she was glad enough to sink down behind the rocks, where she wouldn't be able to see what was happening.

But she could still hear. Henry Wilshire was a very different sort from the hapless lawyer lying unconscious behind them. He was at least as well trained and as experienced in the ways of death as Owen himself. And he possessed the same kind of instincts that warned him of approaching danger.

Because of that, he approached the cave cautiously, something causing him to stop before stepping into the cave. He reached into the holster concealed by his jacket, drawing from it an automatic pistol. With the safety off he moved at last toward the cave. "Pierce...?"

No answer. Only the sound of the wind blowing from hidden sources. That was wrong. He had expected to hear the lawyer mouthing off to the girl, perhaps even to hear the poor sod finally getting what he so obviously wanted from her. That wouldn't have bothered him; he might even have enjoyed having her afterward. But the silence, that troubled him greatly.

"Pierce...?"

A pebble rolled somewhere nearby. Wilshire jumped, his finger tightening on the trigger. He forced himself to wait, giving his eyes time to adjust to the dimness.

Owen felt him coming. In sinew and muscle long trained to violence, he felt him. He spared one last look at the rocks that sheltered Gwen and allowed himself the luxury of a quick prayer that she would have the sense to stay where she was. Then he moved.

Wilshire was good. He had been in the game since he'd turned sixteen, originally in the secret training camps of Ulster, but graduating quickly to more advanced studies in the Middle East and elsewhere. No one knew just how many men he had killed, some at a distance, a dozen or so close up.

His teeth were bared in a grin as he took aim at the shadow moving toward him. He would shoot to wound, not kill. That would come later, with the girl watching.

The first bullet caught him in the right shoulder. Raw, hot pain shot down toward the hand that held the gun. Almost any other man would have dropped it, but Wilshire was as divorced from his own body's suffering as from anyone else's. What he felt was mainly shock.

Wilshire wondered who the hell he was up against. Not Pierce; the lawyer would never dare turn against him, and besides, mindful of the strict gun control laws, he didn't carry a weapon. His bet was that the intruder was the girl's neighbor, the only other person who lived nearby. But what the hell was a supposedly law-abiding Welshman doing with a gun every bit as illegal and lethal as his own?

All this passed through his mind in an instant as he reacted instinctively, flinging himself onto the sandy ground and crawling behind the nearest shelter. Gingerly he transferred the gun to his left hand, taking for granted the hard-earned ability to shoot with either.

Owen had deliberately fired to wound, though for different reasons than Wilshire would have. He was still hoping to be able to bring both men in for questioning, though he realized that the odds of that were rapidly diminishing. Particularly since it was not simply him against Wilshire. He had to protect Gwen at all costs.

But he had miscalculated. Whether from the years away from the turmoil of the world, or whether from his distraction over Gwen, he had not considered that Wilshire might be carrying another kind of weapon.

The explosion took him by surprise. The shock wave threw him onto the ground and momentarily knocked the breath from him. Dust and rock were still falling when he lifted his head to perceive in an instant the cleverness of what the other man had done.

The entrance to the cave was now sealed, brought down by a sample of plastique that had probably been no larger than a child's fist. Wilshire probably routinely carried it in his bag of devil's tricks. He had taken a desperate but brilliant gamble in using it, deliberately trapping his adversary where he might be picked off at leisure.

Except that Owen had no intention of being so easily caught. Barely had the reverberations from the explosion begun to settle than he was on his feet.

Gwen had not made a sound. She crouched white faced and silent behind the rocks. He grabbed her arm without a word and half dragged, half pushed her into the darkness.

Chapter 16

They were past the packing crates loaded with weapons and deeper into the cave when they felt the rumbling. It began slowly, as though the earth were waking from sleep, but it grew quickly in intensity.

Owen stopped, all his senses straining. He was aware of Wilshire behind them, stalking in the darkness, intent on killing. But another, far more potent force impinged on his consciousness. Something he could not comprehend, but that was nonetheless there. Something that made the hair rise on the back of his neck and sent cold fingers of primitive awe shimmering over his skin.

"What could it be?" Gwen whispered. They were holding on to each other as the ground shook beneath

them and the very walls of the cave seemed to ripple.
"An earthquake?"

Owen shook his head. "No, I've been through
those. They don't feel like this."

"It wasn't so strong the other times."

"We're closer to the source," he said. "Whatever
it is."

And they had no choice but to go even closer. His
arm was tight around her waist as they made their way
over the pitching ground. He didn't dare turn on the
flashlight that would give away their position to Wilshire, but it didn't seem to be necessary. After a moment he realized that the passage they were following
was becoming gradually brighter.

Gwen noticed it at the same instant. Hope trembled in her voice as she said, "Daylight?"

"It can't be. We're moving downward." Besides,
the light wasn't the golden color of the sun. It had a
hard, crystalline quality he couldn't explain, though
he tried to. "Phosphorescence, maybe, since we're
near the sea."

Gwen seized on the explanation, if only because it
was something familiar in a situation that was rapidly
spinning out of her grasp.

Yet, paradoxically, she was swiftly regaining control of herself. Her initial shock, brought on by a violence so foreign to her experience, was fading. With
the great survival skill of the human mind, she was
adjusting to changing circumstances.

"What Wilshire did was crazy," she said. "He's trapped himself in here as surely as he's trapped us."

Owen nodded, pleased but hardly surprised that she had grasped that essential point. "He must know another way out. You suspected there might be a connection to the house."

"No wonder they wanted it so badly," she murmured.

"You realize he'll have to get past us to get out."

She nodded, her face pale in the cold light. "And you intend to stop him."

"He's wounded, which will make it easier. But he's probably also carrying additional explosives." He wished he could have spared her that knowledge, but he had to believe that the more information she had, the better the chance of her surviving.

"Gwen," he added quietly, "I'm going to hold him off here. I want you to go on ahead and find the other exit. Find it and use it."

"No." That was all, a single word, but it reverberated between them with a force at least as great as the mysterious tremors.

"Don't be—"

"I'm not leaving you." When he would have argued she held up a hand. "Listen to me. I know what you're proposing is sensible, but this is all tied up with my family, my heritage, and I'm not leaving you to deal with it alone."

"All that's involved here is Wilshire."

"You don't really believe that."

The shadow of a smile gentled his gaze. "Are you telling me you believe in the dragon?"

"I don't know what I believe," she told him, "except that we have to fight this together."

"Not Wilshire," he said. "I'll take care of him. You stay out of sight."

Reluctantly Gwen agreed. She let Owen leave her behind an outcrop where she was protected from the glaring light. She was reassured to notice that the tremors had decreased somewhat.

Owen's attention was focused on the shadow he saw flitting from rock to rock at the edges of the lit passage. Wilshire was being very cautious. Undoubtedly he couldn't explain the source of the light any more than Owen could, but it would put him even more on his guard.

Owen fully grasped the other man's dilemma. If he used additional explosives he would risk bringing down a landslide that could block his own escape. If he didn't, he had to come closer and risk exposing himself in order to get a clear shot.

Meanwhile Owen waited. He was by nature a patient man. That had been one of his greatest strengths when he lived in Wilshire's world. Lately he had turned that patience to more constructive pursuits, the restoration of the monastery, for example. But he remembered well enough how to wait for more deadly purposes.

Unmoving, his hand steady on the gun, he breathed slowly and regularly. There was no doubt in him, no hesitation. An opportunity would present itself soon enough.

Wilshire did not have the same mentality. He was too frightened, too impulsive, to wait. He knew only how to attack, not how to defend, because he had never recognized anything worth protecting.

His shoulder had not stopped bleeding, and already his entire right arm down to the hand was numb. A sense of fearful urgency gripped him. He had to get away—from the cave, the strange light, the throat-burning sense of terror.

He fired randomly, splintering the rock not far from Owen's head. At that moment he was exposed. Owen raised his weapon, took careful aim and fired.

He missed. It wasn't surprising, since Wilshire had correctly anticipated his response and dodged back out of sight. But each man now knew where the other was, and the stakes had just been raised to deadly heights.

Owen knew that he had to move. From where he was, Wilshire could risk using one of the explosive caps and still leave himself room to get away. For Owen, moving out from behind the rock would make him an easy target, while staying where he was would invite disaster.

He took a deep breath, crouched and prepared to run. Even as he did so a soft plop sounded nearby. He looked down, saw the small round cap with its lethal packing and launched himself into space.

The explosion wasn't as large as the one before— Wilshire wasn't up to taking quite that much of a chance—but its force was enough to hurl Owen forward. His body seemed to slam up against a wall of resistance, which was no more than air transformed by his own speed into a potentially deadly substance. The breath was knocked from him, lights whirled before his eyes, and he felt the sickening sensation that precedes the loss of consciousness.

Only by exerting the sheer force of his immensely powerful will did he manage to avoid slipping into the beckoning darkness. As it was, he was barely aware of hitting the ground and rolling. Instinct took over to keep him moving as Wilshire moved in for the kill.

He had a clear shot at Owen. From behind the rocks where she had hidden, Gwen saw that. She cried out, not caring if she was discovered, and without thought threw herself toward Owen. She was thinking only of shielding him with her own body, but what Wilshire saw were two ready targets instead of one. He was smiling as he stepped forward, intending to finish them both off.

A roar filled the cave, as if a freight train were rushing past only a few feet away. Locked in Owen's arms, Gwen screamed.

"What in God's name...?" Owen murmured. He tried to look up, but swirling smoke obscured his vision. Then a rush of heat struck him, and he instinctively ducked his head.

Long moments passed. Gwen and Owen clung together, each other's only shelter in a world gone mad. He tried with all the weight and strength of his powerful body to spare her the worst, but they were spinning out of control, rolling across the floor of the cave and bumping roughly down a sharp-edged incline that finally left them bruised and breathless in the sudden silence.

With Gwen beneath him, his hand cupping the back of her head to hold her firmly to him, Owen looked up cautiously. He could see very little. The strange light was fading, but he was able to make out the slope down which they had fallen.

"I'll be damned," he murmured under his breath.

"What is it?" Gwen croaked. Her throat felt swollen almost shut, though from the smoke or from simple terror she couldn't tell.

"A staircase cut into the rock. People have definitely been here."

She turned her head to look, but he jerked her back against his chest. "Don't," he said. "There's something else."

"W-what...?"

"Wilshire...at the top of the stairs. You don't need to see him."

In fact, he was determined that she wouldn't. The sight was revolting enough to him. What was left of the terrorist was nothing more than the charred husk of a man.

"There must have been another explosion," Gwen said as Owen lifted her to her feet, keeping her back to the stairs.

Owen kept his sudden thought to himself. If what they had heard had been another explosion, there should have been nothing left of Wilshire. But what else could have so severely burned him?

Another staircase about fifty yards opposite the first one led up into the storeroom beneath Myrddin's Rock. A section of the old stone wall gave way to reveal a hidden door. They stumbled through it, and it swung shut behind, but not before Owen thought to jam a length of wood into the opening.

Gwen remembered little of the next few hours. Owen insisted that she drink a stiff whiskey while he called Cardiff. Stern-faced men came in helicopters, landing on the lawn outside the house. They talked with Owen and went down into the cave. Wilshire's body was removed, decently covered, on a stretcher. Daniel was taken away in handcuffs. Miraculously, he had survived without injury, returning to befuddled consciousness even as the authorities swooped down on him.

A soft-spoken man took a statement from Gwen under Owen's watchful eye. She told him the basics of what she had seen and heard, nothing else. No suppositions, no mysteries.

Much later she and Owen were curled together in his bed beneath the benevolent eye of the maiden in the tapestry. They had showered together, washing the grime from each other with tender hands. There was nothing sexual about their touching. That would come later; this was the time for simply holding.

Beneath the cool sheets and soft blankets, naked in his arms, she felt infinitely safe. The terrible experiences of a few hours before might almost have been a dream.

"I don't suppose," Gwen said quietly, "that we'll ever know what really happened down there."

"Perhaps not," Owen acknowledged. "But," he added a moment later, "it might be well worth trying to find out."

She propped herself up on an elbow and looked at his dearly beloved face. Absently her fingers traced the scar that crossed his brow. "What do you mean?"

He touched a finger to the tempting fullness of her lower lip. "We both felt something down there that neither of us can explain."

"The men who were here think they can. Wilshire was killed by an explosion. The sound we heard was exaggerated by the cave walls, which in effect turned the cave into an echo chamber. The light must have filtered in from boreholes leading to the outside."

"They have to believe that," he said. "We can face the possibility that there's more to it."

Their eyes met and held as she murmured, "The legend?"

Slowly he nodded.

She sighed deeply. "It's too much to believe."

Against her hair he murmured softly, "So is love, yet it exists. It's the greatest magic of all."

Gwen could only agree. With him, she had found more than she had ever hoped to know, more happiness, more security and more strength to confront the challenges of the future.

Quietly she said, "It will take special people to find out the truth about Myrddin's Rock."

He nodded. "And it won't happen quickly. But someday..."

Gwen smiled against his skin. She could see the way it would be. Together she and Owen would make of Myrddin's Rock a sanctuary. She would keep faith with her family's legacy and at the same time build the life she wanted for herself. A life with a man for whom she felt a love that transcended both past and future, a love that promised to endure for all eternity.

Beneath the bed the floor reverberated gently. She and Owen exchanged a smile and moved more closely into each other's arms.

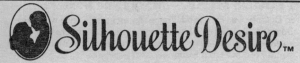

Silhouette Intimate Moments

COMING
NEXT MONTH

#197 FOOL'S MUSIC—Mary Lynn Baxter

Lauren DeCoty was on a modeling assignment in France when she was abducted. To Lauren's horror, one of her kidnappers was Ry Kincaid—her first and only love. Ry promised to protect her, but who would keep her from losing her heart—again?

#198 COMMAND PERFORMANCE—
Nora Roberts

Eve always thought of Alexander de Cordina as a fairy-tale prince from a magical kingdom. Then she discovered that Alexander was a man of flesh and blood and passionate feelings—and that the land of happily ever after held a danger that was frighteningly real.

#199 THE DREAMING—Amanda Stevens

Except in her dreams, Toni Sinclair had no time for romance—until she went on vacation in Egypt. There she met David Spaulding, then found herself fleeing from an attacker, not sure if she could trust the man she loved.

#200 MISTRESS OF CLIFF HOUSE—
Jeanne Stephens

In the past, Cassie Underwood had loved visiting Cliff House, but this time her nights were haunted by footsteps, and her days were disturbed by Daniel Reardon. Cassie suspected Daniel of theft: her grandmother's papers and jewels were missing—and so was Cassie's heart.

AVAILABLE THIS MONTH:

#193 KISS OF THE DRAGON
Barbara Faith

#194 LEGACY
Maura Seger

#195 THE GENUINE
ARTICLE
Katheryn Brett

#196 GYPSY DANCER
Kathleen Creighton

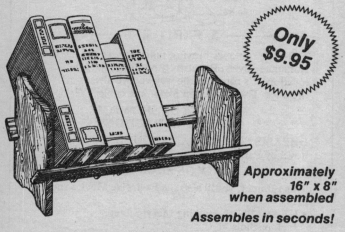